"Fiction is the truth inside the lie."
– Stephen King

DRIVEN

A Screenplay

By Daniel John Carey

ISBN: 978-1-884702-48-8
First published: 2025

Published by: Oakonic

DRIVEN

A struggling young screenwriter attempts to save a
reclusive actress after she undergoes failed cosmetic
eyelid surgery as – unknown to the screenwriter – she
becomes obsessed with stalking and taking revenge
against the womanizing doctor who ruined her.

"All readers come to fiction as willing accomplices to your lies. Such is the basic goodwill contract made the moment we pick up a work of fiction."
– Steve Almond

The Published Script

This script is not in the industry standard screenplay format. It has been adjusted for publishing.

Because some people read screenplays as some others read novels – strictly for entertainment – this script is being made available in print.

Screenplays often bump around Hollywood for years, before they are optioned or purchased. Even after being optioned or purchased they may not be produced – or can take years to go into production.

Before filming, screenplays often are rewritten to display the talents of the leading actors who are cast. This could result in a script vastly different from the original screenplay. What you hold in your hands is the version of the script the screenwriter wrote.

Publishing this screenplay allows people interested in entering screenplay contests, and other showcases, a way to read what could be considered a top entry – as this script has been.

In 2016, Carey founded the Screenwriting Tribe script incubation workshop in Los Angeles, which has over 1,000 members. He also polishes screenplays for producers, and works one-on-one with some writers. He wrote the *Screenplay Repair Manual*, which has been used as a text in film schools.

Genesis

Years ago, I read a news story about a woman who was extremely unhappy with her facelift, and she ended up stalking the surgeon. Then I noticed other stories of cosmetic patients doing awful things to doctors, including some doctors being murdered, and one of the doctors vanishing, never to be found.

There was also a cosmetic surgeon in California who was ambushed in the parking lot of a restaurant. Apparently he had botched numerous patients, including some with wealth. The killer could have been any of a variety of people, or one of their family members, or friends, or a hired hit. I met one of his patients, who told me about how the doctor botched her cosmetic surgery. She smiled as she told me about how nobody knows who murdered him, and that the investigation became so expensive and time consuming detectives stopped trying to figure out the puzzle. Decades later, it remains a cold case.

I had a neighbor in the film industry who wanted to get her eyelids done. She asked me if I could take her to the surgery appointment, then care for her for a couple of days as she knew I was spending my days writing.

My mind started to tick, mixing truth and fiction. I started typing, and this script was born.

As the script was passed around Hollywood, I met various directors, managers, producers, production executives, and actors.

At one point an actor was interested in playing the doctor role. A certain actress of the same level was interested in playing the actress role. I thought the casting was perfect, and the script would soon be going into pre-production.

Then… the actor decided he didn't want to play another doctor. The actress then lost interest as she was only interested in working with the actor.

Another well-known actor was interested in it, and also decided against it. He also didn't want to play another doctor role, as he wanted to diversify his filmography. He was kind enough to send me a handwritten letter about how much he liked the script.

Like other screenplays, this one has been knocking around Hollywood for a while. As I'm writing this in the summer of 2025, more people are considering the script for production.

I know people who are not in the film industry, but who read screenplays for entertainment the way other people read novels. People I know who are not in the industry keep asking me to read this script. These things are what gave me the idea of making the script available in a printed format. At least people can enjoy the script in this form. And maybe one day we will be able to watch it on the big screen.

If you have never read a screenplay, know that a screenplay simply presents what is seen, and what is heard. A character's fears, regrets, plans, wants, and memories – and otherwise their thoughts – are the type of information found in a novel. Screenplays usually avoid wordy, novelesque writing – especially about what a character is thinking. One goal of writing a screenplay is to be minimalist, with strong subtext.

I hope you enjoy *Driven*.

Daniel John Carey

NOTES:

- This is a twisted script largely consisting of a screenplay within a screenplay. At first, viewers aren't meant to notice.

- "Duke's script" scenes are from a script he is writing.

- "Real life" scenes are from Duke's real life he's using to distort into the story he is writing.

- Visuals (including sudden wardrobe changes that might appear to be mistakes) will help viewers to detect something is amiss as a puzzle is presented for them to figure out.

- Each paragraph of description is meant to be a different camera angle

— EXT. means exterior = outdoors.

— INT. means interior = indoors.

— SUPER: means words are to be "superimposed" on the screen for viewers to read.

— If dialogue has double hyphen after it, this means the character's dialogue is being interrupted by the other character's dialogue.
     As in:

               BARBARA
I was going to --

               CANDICE
-- You were not!

DRIVEN

BLACK SCREEN - YEAR 2000 — CALIFORNIA

Sounds of an out-of-breath man and crunching gravel as he
apparently runs. Sounds of his breathing and feet landing
on the gravel are interrupted by...

Horrifying, drawn-out screams of a woman. These are taken
over by...

the lengthy screech of tires on pavement that turn into...
screechy violin music. It mildly becomes less screechy,
and turns elegant and fades away into...

a darkly haunting melody played on a piano.

FADE IN

INT. L.A. MANSION - NIGHT (DUKE'S SCRIPT)

A man's fingers dance across piano keys played by...

suited, tan, fit BERNARD WALTERS (50). An self-impressed
arrogance about him.

Wine is poured by a hot butler for a Botoxed, older lady.

Well-dressed, rich, older men and their vaguely younger,
cosmetically-enhanced spouses listen to the piano.

WALTER'S FINGERS: Play the piano. His fingers turn into...

INT. DUKE'S STUDIO APARTMENT - NIGHT (REAL LIFE)

Young black man's fingers type on a laptop.

ON THE LAPTOP SCREEN: A screenplay as dialogue is typed...

"Alicia: Scream all you want. Nobody can hear you."

The screenwriter is sincere-faced DUKE (early 20s),
dreadlocks, in a T-shirt and board shorts, at a crappy
desk in the dumpy apartment.

On the basic bed reclines hippyish JENNIFER (20s), who reads a book and smokes a joint. She notices...

Duke stares as he has stopped typing.

She straddles him and blows pot smoke into his mouth as he inhales. She giggles. He exhales the smoke.

> JENNIFER
> I cast a spell. Do not linger. You must tell your story, through your fingers.

They kiss. They eye each other as she gets off him.

He looks to the keyboard. Stares. Lifts his hands.

LAPTOP KEYBOARD: His fingers land on keys. He types.

INT. WALTERS' POSH BEACH HOUSE FOYER - DAY (DUKE'S SCRIPT)

SUPERIMPOSE: "Months later."

The point of a knife hovers close to the worried eye of Walters as he's in a fully hooded, black bondage suit, the mouth unzipped as he lies face-up on the marble floor.

The other hand of the unseen woman holds a phone to his ear.

> ALICIA (O.S.)
> (angry whisper)
> Do. Not. Fuck. Up.

His eyes worry. The other end of the phone is heard ringing.

INT. PSYCHOTHERAPY OFFICE - DAY (FLASHBACK - DUKE'S SCRIPT)

SUPER: "Months earlier."

DR. LINDER (60s), distinguished with smart glasses and curiously messy hair. She sits in an upholstered chair.

> LINDER
> (calmly to unseen patient)
> Would you like it darker in here?

She looks beside her. Presses a button. Curtains close.

> LINDER
> In what way do you feel it was self-perpetuated?

She waits.

                    LINDER
          Alicia? Are you sleeping? I can't see past
          your sunglasses.

Linder checks her watch. Boredom.

INT. POSH BEACH HOUSE FOYER - DAY (DUKE'S SCRIPT)

Two syringes hang stuck in his neck and bare back...

as sweaty, tan, shirtless Walters struggles to crawl
across the marble floor. He's in jog shorts and wears a
fanny pack. From the fanny pack, he struggles to pull a
flip phone.

As her upper body and face remain unseen, the woman's foot
in sports shoes kicks away his phone.

He turns onto his back.

                    WALTERS
               (drugged)
          Alicia... What do you want from me?

His eyes plead. He collapses back, passed out.

INT. STEPHEN'S OFFICE - DAY (DUKE'S SCRIPT)

A wall-mounted, silent T.V. spews year 2000 celebrity
gossip crap.

A line of cocaine is snorted from the desk into a rolled
dollar into the nose of cynical-eyed, tightly suited
talent manager STEPHEN (mid-30s). Posh haircut.

He turns his chair to stare at passing traffic on Wilshire
Blvd. Cocaine powder on his nostrils. His eyes glass over
as the cocaine hits.

OFFICE DOOR: Opens. Sharply dressed, flamboyant TOBY CHO
(20s), enters with a to-go coffee cup he places on the
desk.

                    TOBY
          Coffee?... You're welcome... How about we
          forget Alicia. Let's focus on your other
          clients. Shall we?

Stephen spins the chair to face Toby. His glassy eyes
glare.

Toby smiles. Flirtatiously winks.

                    STEPHEN
          You're fired. Get the fuck out.

> TOBY
> As a junior agent, you can only request a
> different assistant, who will also hate you.
> So, suck it.

> STEPHEN
> Find Alicia.

> TOBY
> How? With my magical powers?

Toby pretends to wave a magical wand. Stops. Scoffs.

> TOBY
> You have cocaine on your nose.

Stephen tastes the coffee.

> TOBY
> I'll go distribute flyers all over Hollywood.
> Actress missing. For a fun time, call Stephen.
> Bring blow.

Toby turns, purposefully swishes as he exits. Door slams.

Stephen stares. Wipes his nose of cocaine. Licks his
fingers.

**EXT. OCEAN CLIFF/BIG SUR - DAY (REAL LIFE MIXED WITH
DUKE'S SCRIPT)**

In fog, ferocious waves crash against the cliffside rocks.

His dreadlocks flip in the blustery wind as weary Duke
stands on the cliff. His gaze set out on the ocean. In an
old leather jacket and jeans. He turns to see his
imagination as...

a Mercedes speed off the cliff, and plunge into the ocean.

Duke stares out at the ocean. Takes a big breath. Lets it
out. Leans down, takes up sand in his hands and stands. He
clasps the sand in his fists held out to the ocean.

> DUKE
> (recites Poe's "Dream within a Dream")
> I stand amid the roar. Of a surf-tormented
> shore, and hold within my hand grains of
> golden sand. How few! Yet how they creep,
> through my fingers to the deep.

He tosses the fists of sand over the cliff.

                              DUKE
                    (loudly, his own words)
          In the dark, they will watch. My dreams, they
          will see. Above this sea, I commit to me. It
          will be. It will be.

He determinedly stares at the ocean. Tears fall.

**EXT. OCEAN/BIG SUR BEACH - DAY (DREAM SEQUENCE/DUKE'S
SCRIPT)**

A wave forms, curls, and flattens into foamy surf.

The surf retreats from rough sand as ocean sounds dreamily
mix with giggles of an unseen boy and girl.

On the sand stands haggard ISABELLA (80), garish makeup,
tattered gown, holds a golden award statue and the leash
of...

a decrepit dog in a tutu, eye shadow, nail polish. It
squats.

                          ISABELLA
                    (odd accent)
          Go ahead. Go poop for mummy.

Near the dog, a garden rake is dragged by a raggedy man
with no eyes, nose, or mouth. The mew of a cat is heard.

THE RAKE: Continues past a puddle that transforms into...

IN OCEAN WATER - KELP FOREST - NIGHT (DREAM/DUKE'S SCRIPT)

Kelp sways in the gentle current. Skidding tires and a
woman's scream are heard. A plunge disturbs the kelp.

Some sort of vehicle sinks through the kelp. Headlights
fade.

In the water-filled vehicle, an obscure person with long
blond hair struggles to break a window.

FADE TO BLACK

SUPER ON BLACK: "Los Angeles, July 2000." (DUKE'S SCRIPT)

Dreamy sounds fade in and out: Cat mews. Metal clangs
metal. A phone rings. Surf. A plunge. Muffled deep water
sounds.

                          ISABELLA (O.S.)
          Go poop for mummy. There you go. That's a good
          sized one. Lovely.

A cat is heard mewing.

FADE IN:

INT. ALICIA'S BEDROOM - DAY (DUKE'S SCRIPT)

In bed sits worried ALICIA DOVER (mid 30s) in a posh robe. She gathers her long blond hair. A small but obvious scar on one eyelid. She sadly looks around the room of grand, old furniture.

She cries. The phone rings. A cat, WICKED, hops onto the bed. Mews.

The answering machine clicks on.

> **ALICIA/ANSWERING MACHINE (V.O.)**
> Hello, beautiful person. Leave a message.

> **STEPHEN/ANSWERING MACHINE (V.O.)**
> Hey babe, Larry Valsa saw an advance copy of the film. His people asked your age. I said twenty-five. So, dress young for the audition. K? Call me.

She weeps as she pets the cat as it purrs. Then, dreadfully saddened, Alicia deeply cries.

INT. ACTING CLASS - DAY (REAL LIFE)

A mix of students (late teens to 70s) sit in a circle. Among them...

Duke attempts to cry. He glances next to him at a SNOB GIRL (early 20s), who cries.

Duke tries harder to cry. Doesn't. Frustrated.

A passionately energetic ACTING COACH (70s), observes.

> **ACTING COACH**
> Duke, relax your face. Allow your breath to guide your emotions.

The man next to Duke cries deeply. Duke side eyes him.

> **ACTING COACH**
> Think of your childhood. When you felt scared. Someone harmed you. Maybe a bully. Or, a mean adult.

The man cries disturbingly harder.

> **ACTING COACH**
> Call out for your mommy!

The actors whine for their mommies as...

Duke sits frustrated.

> **ACTING COACH**
> (to Duke)
> Well. Not everyone can cry on cue.

The actors simmer down. Some giggle. Others wipe tears.

Snob Girl dries her tears. Looks at Duke askance.

> **DUKE**
> I'd much rather be a screenwriter.

She rolls her eyes. Crosses a leg away from him.

> **ACTING COACH**
> (as if profound)
> Okay. For your next exercise, think of an
> invisible butterfly. One you've never seen.

INT. TRENDY GYM - KICKBOXING CLASS - DAY (REAL LIFE)

Dance music blasts. Her sweaty hair clings to her back as
Alicia attacks a kickboxing bag in sync with the music
among...

trendy gym members who attack kickboxing bags.

A muscular, tattooed, female kickboxing COACH passes
Alicia.

> **COACH**
> (shouts)
> Kick it like you mean it!

The Coach wanders the room.

> **COACH**
> Twenty jumping jacks!

Some members obey. Alicia gathers her towel and backpack.

A couple of sweaty women talk as they cattily watch
Alicia.

Alicia notices them, flips her sweaty hair, and exits.

INT. HOSPITAL PATIENT ROOM - DAY (REAL LIFE)

Two concerned nurses whisper to each other. Monitors beep.

Asleep on the bed is Alicia. Badly bruised eyes. Nasty, bare wound stitched across her forehead. An I.V. attached to her arm.

Next to the bed stands distressed Duke, in a hospital gown, I.V. attached to his arm, he's on the edge of tears.

A somber doctor enters. He hauntedly stares at Alicia as if at a loss of what to do or say. His eyes well with tears. Perhaps too many tears.

Tears streak Duke's face. His breath heaves. He cries deeply.

> **JILL THE A.D. (O.S.)**
> End rehearsal! Final looks!

A makeup artist approaches the doctor, dries his tears, and powders his chin.

FILM SET VIDEO VILLAGE

The geeky dweeb director, MARK (30s), sits next to the poker-faced SCRIPT SUPERVISOR busy making notes.

Dr. Walters is in a jacket as he sits next to Mark.

> **MARK**
> (to Walters)
> F.X. did a great job with the wounds, huh, doc?

> **WALTERS**
> Even I couldn't do a better job.

Mark and Walters eye the camera monitors in front of them.

> **MARK**
> Almost done with this actress. Thank god.

> **SCRIPT SUPERVISOR**
> (continues on her notes)
> Her Sharon Grock film opening this summer is supposed to be fantastic.

> **MARK**
> "Driven"? Please. Just because Sundance loved it doesn't mean flyover people will.
> (cynically)
> Her and Sharon Grock on the same set. Sounds like a nightmare.

HOSPITAL ROOM

A handsome camera operator, GREGORY (30), tests the angle of the lens he focuses on Duke.

VIDEO VILLAGE

The stern A.D., JILL (30s), approaches video village.

> **JILL**
> Quiet on set!... Roll cameras!

> **GREGORY (O.S.)**
> Rolling!

HOSPITAL ROOM

CAMERA ASSISTANTS hold up clap boards for the two cameras.

> **CAMERA ASSISTANT A**
> A-mark.

> **CAMERA ASSISTANT B**
> B-mark.

The Camera Assistants clap the boards and step away. A boom operator holds the mic over Alicia's bed.

> **BOOM OPERATOR**
> Sync!

> **JILL (O.S.)**
> Background!

The nurses get busy adjusting I.V.s, etc.

Alicia's hand is held by Duke, as he weeps.

> **MARK (O.S.)**
> Action!

The somber "doctor" actor enters. Begins to weep.

He approaches sleeping Alicia.

She barely opens her eyes.

> **ALICIA**
> (struggles to speak)
> I... survived?... Am I... alive?

She cries. Looks to Duke. He cries, deeply. Alicia closes her eyes.

Duke cries harder. The doctor grasps Duke's shoulder.

VIDEO VILLAGE

Mark hops from his chair.

>   MARK
>   Good Alicia! Cut. Print. That's all we needed
>   for that.

>   JILL
>   Check the gate!

HOSPITAL ROOM

Duke and Alicia giggle. A prop person removes their I.V.s.

>   ALICIA
>   Duke, you cry so well.

>   DUKE
>   Thanks. Gosh, and all that stuff.

>   JILL (O.S.)
>   Clear set. Crew has it.

The nurses and doctor clear the set. Duke follows.

Gregory approaches Alicia.

>   GREGORY
>   (offers helpful hand)
>   Miss Dover.

Alicia takes his hand as she scoots from the bed. Gregory
is stopped by a crew member who has a question.

Alicia continues out, but stops as she spies...

BEHIND THE HOSPITAL SET

Mark talks with Jill.

>   MARK
>   Larry Valsa wants her for his film? She's too
>   old. The character's in her twenties. Alicia
>   looks forty.

Jill notices Alicia. Mark turns to see...

Alicia gives him a hurtful look, and storms away.

>   MARK
>   (whispers to Jill)
>   Shit! Did she hear me?

Jill shrugs "who cares."

                    MARK
We're nearly done with that nut case, anyway.
But, hey, her being in Valsa's film could help
ours.

                    JILL
True.

Mark walks away. Jill rolls her eyes.

EXT. SOUND STAGE - DAY - CONT. (REAL LIFE)

A badly damaged Mercedes that looks as if it had been
underwater sits near the basecamp where various P.A.s
pass.

Still in the hospital gown, Duke stares at the car. He
holds a thick book with a "how to write screenplays"
title.

INT./EXT. STAGE DOOR - DAY (REAL LIFE)

Alicia in her hospital gown and fake facial wounds catches
up with Gregory as they exit to the base camp of
production trailers, near where P.A.s and crew buzz about.

                    ALICIA
Has an actress ever murdered a director?

Gregory turns to her as they stop.

                    GREGORY
The cameraman was nice, wasn't he?

He teasingly leans in to coax her. They sneak a kiss.

Duke approaches as he holds the screenwriting book.

                    ALICIA
Nice dress there, Duke.

                    DUKE
I wouldn't be in the hospital, if you hadn't
crashed our car.

                    ALICIA
You survived. So, get over it.
     (to Gregory)
Gregory, you've met Duke. He's worked on my
last two films. I've hired him to be my
assistant.

                    DUKE
Oh, hey, when are they gonna film us crashing
the car?

> GREGORY
>
> We're not filming that. It's only gonna show
> the car being pulled from the ocean.

> DUKE
>
> Ohhh. I was thinking it would be a big,
> dramatic scene.

Gregory looks at his phone. Puts it to his ear.

> GREGORY
>   (into phone)
> Hello.

Gregory walks off with phone to ear.

> DUKE
>   (waves bye to Gregory)
> Yeah. Nice meeting you, too, buddy.

Alicia giggles.

> DUKE
>
> Isn't he way younger than you?

> ALICIA
>
> What?
>   (pokes his side)
> Don't be such an ageist bitch!

He retreats. She attempts to tickle him, he fends her off.
She stops as she sees...

BASE CAMP TRAILERS: A large, sweaty, suited man, LARRY
VALSA (60), with two assistant types, approaches a
trailer.

Alicia hides behind Duke.

> DUKE
>
> What's going on?

> ALICIA
>
> Larry Valsa. The producer. He's at Mark's
> trailer. He can't see me like this.

TRAILER: Mark happily opens the door for Larry. The two
assistants help Larry struggle up the stairs.

> ALICIA
>   (to Duke)
> He wants me for his next film.

Alicia takes Duke's hand. They nearly walk into Walters as
he rises from a chair, where Walters' jacket hangs.

                    WALTERS
How're those stitches holding up?

                    ALICIA
A bit itchy, actually.

She peels the prosthetic wound halfway off. It flops
around.

                    ALICIA
There. All pretty now.

Duke and Alicia giggle. Walters' eyes linger on her,
awkwardly.
                    ALICIA
What kind of doctor are you that you consult
on movie sets?

                    WALTERS
I specialize in cosmetic procedures.

                    DUKE
Like, face lifts, and that kinda --

                    WALTERS
-- Facial rejuvenation, nasal refinement.
Breast enhancement.

                    DUKE
That's bank. You must live in a mansion.

                    ALICIA
          (to Walters)
Excuse him, he's young.

                    WALTERS
Only a house on Santa Monica beach. I like
going for a jog on the sand every morning.

Walters holds out a business card for Alicia.

                    WALTERS
In case you ever need anything.

She takes it. Walters steps away as he dials his phone.

She considers the business card.

                    DUKE
Creeeepy. He slices apart people's faces and
sews them back together.

                    ALICIA
How old do I look? Be honest.

                    DUKE
          Fifty... seven?

                    ALICIA
          Asshole.

She takes the jacket from the chair where Walters had sat.

                    DUKE
          What're you doing? That's the creepy doctor's.

She hooks her arm in his and they walk toward her trailer.
She carries the jacket. He carries the screenwriting book.

INT. ALICIA'S TRAILER - MOMENTS LATER (REAL LIFE)

Alicia and Duke enter. She tosses the jacket to a seat,
near where Duke sits.

                    ALICIA
          I don't know what working as my assistant will
          entail. You can start by helping me smoke a
          joint.

She opens a small jar, and removes a joint.

                    DUKE
          You gonna give him his jacket?

                    ALICIA
              (lights the joint)
          It's my jacket. I loaned it to him. He was cold
          on set.

She picks up his book. Reads the back cover.

                    ALICIA
          Another screenwriting book?

She puffs as she sits next to him. He takes the joint and
tokes as she flips through the book.

                    DUKE
          If I wrote a screenplay for you, would you read
          it?

She takes the joint and puffs. Considers him.

                    ALICIA
          I'll read anything you write.

                    DUKE
          A lot of times I base things on people I know.

                    ALICIA
    Write a script about us. Then, you can co-star
    in it.

                    DUKE
    Maybe I'll do that.

                    ALICIA
    Remember, when writing a script, you gotta fuck
    with the audience.

She rips the prosthetic wound from her forehead and
SCREAMS.

                    DUKE
    Actresses are nuts!

She playfully pushes him as she stands.

                    ALICIA
    You can hang out here. I'm gonna go have them
    clean my face.

She hands him the book, and heads out. He ponders.

EXT. HOLLYWOOD BLVD. - DAY (REAL LIFE)

On a crappy motorcycle, Duke stops at a red light.

A woman with impossibly enhanced breasts crosses the
street.

Duke watches her, then looks up to see...

A BILLBOARD: The airbrushed face of a woman. "Have the
face you've always wanted. Lotus Cosmetic Surgery Center."

Duke stares at the billboard. A car horn goes off. He
snaps out of his daydream, and revs away on the
motorcycle.

EXT. SANTA MONICA PIER BAR - NIGHT (DUKE'S SCRIPT)

Young hipsters wait in line as muffled night club music is
heard. Among those in line are Gregory and Alicia.

A doorman checks Gregory's I.D., but does not look at
Alicia's I.D. He nods for her to pass through.

Gregory takes her hand. She frowns as she flips her hair
into the face of the doorman. Amused, he turns to the next
person in line.

INT. PIER BAR - NIGHT (DUKE'S SCRIPT)

The young crowd dances to loud music. Among them...

Alicia and Gregory dance closer and closer to each other.
Sweat streaks their faces. The heat is on.

LADIES ROOM - MINUTES LATER (DUKE'S SCRIPT)

At the mirror, the Snob Girl from Duke's acting class, and
her pretty FRIEND (20s), adjust their hair.

> **FRIEND**
> Did you see that older chick dancing? I think
> she's an actress.

> **SNOB GIRL**
> Yeah. Acting as if she's all young.

Friend exits. A toilet flushes. Alicia exits the stall and
glares at Snob Girl, who nearly trips as she exits.

Alicia washes her hands as she stares in the mirror.

EXT. SANTA MONICA PIER - NIGHT (DUKE'S SCRIPT)

Among random strollers, several people watch their fishing
lines cast into the ocean.

Alicia and Gregory lean on the railing. She pulls him
close. They kiss. A clanging sound of metal hitting metal
is heard. As they embrace, Alicia looks up to a...

FLAG POLE: A metal clasp on a rope clangs against the pole
where a lighted coast guard flag flaps in the breeze.

Alicia remains in Gregory's embrace as she watches the
flag pole. The scar on her eyelid is obvious.

**EXT. BIG SUR FOREST - RAMSHACKLE HOUSE - NIGHT
(FLASHBACK/DUKE'S SCRIPT)**

Terrified and disheveled Alicia, her eyelid bleeding. She
pauses to listen. Silence as she turns to look back to
the...

house in the woods. A dull light is in one window.
Stillness.

She squats next to an old pickup truck. She hammers on
something unseen. Sounds of metal hitting metal.

END FLASHBACK

EXT. PIER - NIGHT (DUKE'S SCRIPT)

A fisherman draws up his line with a struggling fish
hooked.

Alicia and Gregory release their embrace.

> **GREGORY**
> I don't know if I'd eat fish from this water.
> Who knows what's down there.

They gaze down at the...

OCEAN WATER: dark and heaving.

They continue to watch it.

> **ALICIA**
> (as if lost in thought)
> Things people want gone.

He seems humored. She clicks out of her thoughts and holds
onto him, notices his smile and smiles back to lighten up.

> **ALICIA**
> Did you move here from Chicago to work in the
> industry?

> **GREGORY**
> I was already in it. It was time to leave. My
> wife left me for her drug dealer... Now, she's
> a stripper... Sorry, I know that's heavy.

> **ALICIA**
> Where's your son?

> **GREGORY**
> My parents have him so he can finish the school
> year there. They're retiring to Arizona this
> summer. And my son will be here, with me.

She nods thoughtfully. They gaze out to the water.

> **ALICIA**
> I grew up with a single mom after I was ten. We
> lived in a dilapidated house in the forest. She
> didn't trust people... Especially in town.

> **GREGORY**
> In small towns, everyone knows your business.

> **ALICIA**
> Big towns, everyone's lonely.

She snuggles up to him. He kisses her forehead. She pulls him close. He kisses her cheek. They kiss.

Two small boys fishing with their father notice, and giggle.

INT. ALICIA'S BEDROOM - NIGHT (DUKE'S SCRIPT)

Wicked the cat scampers from the room.

On the bed, clothes are shed as Alicia and Gregory go at it. A little rough, she is as aggressive as he is.

More clothes shed. Thrusty kisses.

The blur of skin on skin. Obscured. Breathing blends together. Moans and breathlessness.

MINUTES LATER

Gregory collapses onto the bed as Alicia relaxes onto a pillow. Exhales. She turns to him with a smile.

> **ALICIA**
> Hell, yes.

They snicker. Satisfied. Eyes close. Her breath slows, as does his. She cuddles up to him, drifting into dreamland.

EXT. BIG SUR BEACH - DAY - 1980S (FLASHBACK/DUKE'S SCRIPT)

Happy, out-of-breath, 9-year-old Alicia in raggedy hippy clothes, runs and playfully falls to the sand.

Shaggy-haired LEONARD (14), puts a crab on her stomach.

> **LEONARD**
> He's gonna eat you up.

> **ALICIA**
> I'm not ascared.

They giggle. Alicia sits up, the crab scampers away.

NEARBY ON THE BEACH

With a black eye and bloody nose, hippie MOM (30s), rushes in front of haggard DAD (40s), long blond hair, Hell's Angel type. He drunkenly follows her.

> **MOM**
> You leave them alone.

                              DAD
                         (mockingly)
               Leave them alone. Leave them alone.

Mom rushes toward Alicia and Leonard.

                              MOM
               Run! Run away from him! Now!

Leonard and Alicia scamper backwards. Mom takes Alicia's
hand, and reaches for Leonard's.

Dad whacks Leonard upside the head.

                            ALICIA
               NO DADDY!

Dad grabs Leonard and violently shakes him.

                              DAD
               What were you doing to her?

Dad throws Leonard into the surf. A wave rolls in as
Leonard trudges in from the water.

                              DAD
                         (angrily to Alicia)
               What was he doing to you?

Alicia backs away.

From behind him, Mom with a piece of driftwood, whacks
Dad's head. He turns to her.

She again whacks his head. HARD.

Blood drips from his hair as he stumbles toward her. He
falls. Attempts to get up. Collapses. Blood streams from
his head to the sand.

Mom grabs Alicia's and Leonard's hands. They run.

A wave washes over Dad. Blood streaks the water. Another
wave rolls over him and washes his limp body into the
surf.

Mom, Alicia, and Leonard run. Alicia fearfully looks back.

END FLASHBACK

INT. ALICIA'S BEDROOM - DAY (DUKE'S SCRIPT)

Light streams through the curtains as Gregory gets
dressed.

Alicia sleeps, but lightly moans.

He sits on the bed, gently takes her hand. She jolts awake with frightened eyes.

> **GREGORY**
> It's okay. It's okay.

As she composes herself, he strokes her hair.

> **GREGORY**
> What were you dreaming about?

She lies back down.

> **ALICIA**
> I don't remember.

> **GREGORY**
> Dreams are strange that way.

He buttons his shirt.

> **ALICIA**
> Are you leaving? I'll make breakfast.

> **GREGORY**
> I can't miss my flight.

She brings a leg around him and pulls him to fall on her.

> **GREGORY**
> I'll be back in a week. Or, when they finish filming.

He stands as he holds her hand and leans to kiss her brow.

> **GREGORY**
> (Poe's "A Dream within a Dream")
> Take this kiss upon the brow. And, in parting from you now, thus much let me avow, you are not wrong, who deem that my days have been a dream.

> **ALICIA**
> Yet if hope has flown away. In a night, or in a day. In a vision, or in none. Is it therefor the less gone?

> **GREGORY**
> All that we see or seem, is but a dream within a dream.

They kiss. He takes a last look at her. She reaches for him. He touches her hand, backs away, and exits.

Wicked the cat hops onto the bed. Alicia sadly pets the cat as the door is heard closing.

> **ALICIA**
> (continues the poem)
> While I weep. While I weep! Oh God! Can I not grasp them with a tighter clasp? Oh God! Can I not save one from the pitiless wave? Is all that we see or seem but a dream within a dream?

She weeps.

ALICIA'S BATHROOM - MINUTES LATER (DUKE'S SCRIPT)

Toothpaste is squeezed onto a toothbrush.

Alicia at the mirror brushes her teeth. Stops. Touches the scar on her eyelid. Sadly stares at herself.

INT. DR. LINDER'S OFFICE - DAY (FLASH FORWARD/DUKE'S SCRIPT)

Linder sits as she considers...

Alicia is in dark sunglasses as she's on the sofa.

> **ALICIA**
> (morosely livid)
> I don't understand. Why did he do it? What kind of sick fuck is he?

> **LINDER**
> I can't give you an assessment of his situation. I don't know him.

> **ALICIA**
> How can I ever work like this? Acting is all about the eyes.

Not removing the sunglasses, she wipes away tears.

Unaffected, Linder watches.

END FLASH FORWARD

INT. DOCTOR WALTERS' EXAM ROOM - DAY (DUKE'S SCRIPT)

A distorted reflection of Alicia's face in the chrome of a paper towel dispenser as she checks out her eyelids.

She sits on a chair. Looks over the various framed education certificates, and a framed logo of Lotus Cosmetic Surgery.

The door opens. Walters and his perfect hair enter. He's in a doctor's white jacket, "Dr. Walters" monogrammed on the pocket.

                    WALTERS
          Look who we have here.

                    ALICIA
          Surprised?

                    WALTERS
          Nothing surprises me.

He sits on a wheeled stool in front of her. Awkwardly too close. One of his knees nearly between her legs.

                    WALTERS
               (looks at her breasts)
          What cup size would you like them to be?

                    ALICIA
          I'm here for my eyelids.

He appears confused, takes a second look at her breasts.

She suffers his gaze.

He looks at paperwork on a clipboard.

                    WALTERS
          Are you sure?

                    ALICIA
          Positive.

He scoots his chair even closer, his knee closer to her crotch. He leans in, his face uncomfortably close to hers.

                    WALTERS
          Close your eyes.

He glances at her breasts. He lifts a hand, "accidentally" grazes past one of her breasts.

Her eyes flutter, but close as he touches the skin round her eyes. Her face flushes.

                    WALTERS
               (touches her lids)
          You do have some play here.

He sits back in the squeaky chair. She opens her eyes.

                    WALTERS
          Good to fix it, now. Slight changes early on
          are better than big changes later.

She moves her chair back as he writes on a chart.

                    WALTERS
          How'd you get the scar on your lid?

                    ALICIA
          A fight with my former husband.

He finishes writing.

                    WALTERS
          I can get rid of the scar for you.

                    ALICIA
          Good. Get rid of it.

                    WALTERS
          I can't imagine a lady as pretty as you getting
          in a fight.

She remains poker-faced. He straightens up.

                    WALTERS
          It's a relatively simple procedure. You'll need
          a week of rest. No exercise, sun, smoking, or
          booze.

                    ALICIA
          Okay. And, get rid of the scar.

He winks at her as he stands.

His charm is lost on her.

DR. WALTERS' RECEPTION - MINUTES LATER (DUKE'S SCRIPT)

Next to a grand piano is a huge, impressive fish tank with
multiple colors of fish.

Alicia watches the fish as she's at the reception desk.

The receptionist, ROBIN, a face too worked on to reveal an
age.

                    ROBIN
               (checks the computer)
          He can do it Wednesday, eight A.M. Is that soon
          enough?

Alicia pensively nods.

Robin notices as she types on the computer.

EXT. NEIGHBORHOOD - RANDOM TOWN - DAY (DUKE'S SCRIPT)

A movie crew sets up equipment in front of a house.

Gregory stands on the sidewalk with a phone to his ear.

>   **GREGORY**
> What sort of retreat?

INT./EXT. ALICIA'S CAR (MOVING)/CITY STREETS - CONT. (DUKE'S SCRIPT)

Alicia with phone to ear as she drives.

>   **ALICIA**
> Out in Joshua Tree. A week of yoga. I need to
> rest up, before I start the film. I'll see you
> when you get back.

INT./EXT. ALICIA'S CAR (PARKED)/DUMPY APARTMENT BUILDING - DAY (DUKE'S SCRIPT)

Hip hop music blares on the car speakers as Alicia waits.

>   **ALICIA**
>   (toots the horn)
> C'mon, Duke!

She looks into the lighted visor mirror. Feels the little
scar on her eyelid. The car door opens. She jolts.

>   **ALICIA**
>   (ready to punch)
> Whoa!

Duke gets in.

>   **DUKE**
>   (closes the door)
> Why so jumpy?

>   **ALICIA**
> This neighborhood scares me.

She speeds off as he struggles with the seat belt.

>   **DUKE**
> Your driving scares me.

She smiles, drives faster. He grasps the dashboard.

MINUTES LATER

A joint is puffed by Duke as Alicia is stuck in traffic.

> **DUKE**
> (blows out smoke)
> How do you know he's trustworthy?

She takes the joint.

> **ALICIA**
> It's not like I picked him out of a newspaper
> ad.

She tokes.

> **DUKE**
> Why do people read the newspaper?

He takes the joint. Puffs.

> **ALICIA**
> They like the crime stories. It makes them feel
> like what they've done isn't so bad.

He considers her he puffs the joint.

> **DUKE**
> (exhales)
> The same stories are on the Internet.

> **ALICIA**
> I hate the Internet.

He jokingly sneers at her. She imitates him. He sneers
harder. They laugh. Traffic finally moves.

EXT. VENICE BOARDWALK T-SHIRT BOOTH - DAY (DUKE'S SCRIPT)

The circus of boardwalk people wanders by as two girls
(20s), in bikinis browse a T-shirt rack near where...

Duke tries on wild sunglasses.

> **DUKE**
> (to the girls)
> Hey, baby.

The unimpressed girls walk away.

Duke and Alicia giggle. Duke returns the glasses as...

Alicia glances around, slips a pair of sunglasses into her
purse. She chooses large sunglasses, puts them on. Turns
to him to show him.

                    ALICIA
These. They'll hide my eyes.

                    DUKE
You're really gonna do this? For an acting job
you haven't even got?

                    ALICIA
I'll do anything for that role. And, this
eyelid scar will be gone.

                    DUKE
Anything?

Duke presses his tongue inside the side of his mouth.

                    ALICIA
Ew. Crude. No. I'm a virgin.

                    DUKE
Oh? Is Larry Valsa gonna be your first lover?

                    ALICIA
Yuck. That'd be like licking sidewalk vomit.

She puts her face near his. They jokingly nearly kiss.

                    DUKE
You're my own private movie star.

She quickly kisses his cheek. They take a dance stance, he
tilts her back. He nearly drops her. She squeals. They
laugh.

EXT. ALICIA'S GUEST HOUSE - DAY (DUKE'S SCRIPT)

The door is locked by Alicia. She's in a baseball cap and
big sunglasses. She hands the keys to...

Duke, who follows her down the pathway toward the main
house, an unkept, old mansion. They notice...

Alicia's landlady, haggard Isabella (from earlier dream
sequence), oddly dressed, garish makeup, holds a leash to
an unseen dog rattling in the bushes.

Alicia cautiously takes Duke's hand as they walk.

The rat-like, ancient dog, HAPPY, limps from the bushes in
a tutu and with eye makeup and nail polish.

                    ISABELLA
                (mysterious accent)
Hello. Lovely weather.

                    ALICIA
              (stops at the dog)
          How's Happy today?

                   ISABELLA
              (smile oddly frozen)
          A little better.

Unsurely, Duke keeps a distance as Alicia pets Happy.

                    ALICIA
          You're a good doggy.
              (to Isabella)
          Have a beautiful day.

Alicia follows Duke to...

her car. He gets in the driver's seat. Doors close.

ISABELLA

Watches Duke and Alicia. Then, her dog.

                   ISABELLA
              (to Happy)
          Yes, love. Go poop for mummy.

The creature barely lowers its rigid ass to poo.

INT. DR. LINDER'S OFFICE - DAY (FLASH FORWARD/DUKE'S
SCRIPT)

Black fabric covers Alicia's eyes as she lies on the sofa.

                    ALICIA
          I gave him the benefit of the doubt. But I know
          he brushed against my breast on purpose. He had
          just suggested I get implants. He fucking knew
          I was there for my eyelids. Fucker knew it.

Disinterested, Linder sketches weirdly violent cartoon
characters in a notebook.

END FLASH FORWARD

EXT. MALIBU BEACH - DAY (FLASH BACK/REAL LIFE)

Seagulls scamper in the sand for a piece of bread.

Fully dressed and in jackets, Duke and Alicia in
sunglasses sit on the sand as they eat sandwiches.

                    DUKE
          I thought you were gonna swim.

                    ALICIA
          I don't swim. The ocean scares me.

                    DUKE
          What if you get cast in a movie that requires
          you to swim?

She tosses the rest of the sandwich to the seagulls.

                    ALICIA
          They'll hire a photo double.

                    DUKE
          My acting coach says we should be prepared for
          any scenario.

                    ALICIA
          I never had an acting coach.

                    DUKE
          How'd you learn how to act, then?

                    ALICIA
          You only have to know how to audition.

He finishes his sandwich. She snickers to herself.

                    DUKE
          What?

                    ALICIA
          Just... I don't know... Hollywood. So much
          bullshit.

She gets up and runs through the group of seagulls. They
take flight over the water. She stops to watch.

Duke considers her. Takes a small notebook and pen from
his jacket pocket. Writes.

INT. POSH OFFICE LOBBY - DAY (FLASH FORWARD/DUKE'S SCRIPT)

People in the lounge chairs watch...

Alicia enters in big, dark sunglasses, low-cut, tight
blouse, clingy skirt, and sharp heels as she approaches
the reception desk.

                    ALICIA
               (to receptionist)
          I'm here to see Larry Valsa.

The receptionist nods and searches the computer screen.

VALSA'S OFFICE - LATER (FLASH FORWARD CONT./DUKE'S SCRIPT)

Still in the sunglasses, Alicia is backed against a wall.
Mouth-breather Larry Valsa moves in closely.

                    ALICIA
          (flirtatiously)
     The character wears sunglasses.

                    LARRY
     C'mon, baby. Take them off.

                    ALICIA
     It could be kind of fun.

                    LARRY
     What's that, baby?

                    ALICIA
     With sunglasses on, you could imagine me as
     anyone.

His mouth-breathing gets heavier. He seems to reach for
his zipper.

                    ALICIA
          (whispers)
     Powerful men are so damn hot. Especially you.

He loosens his pants. His breath snorts. She slowly licks
her lips as he seems to masturbate. His eyes aflutter as
he mouth breathes.

She repulsively looks away. He moans, apparently
climaxing.

END FLASH FORWARD

I/E ALICIA'S CAR (MOVING)/DRIVEWAY - DAY (DUKE'S SCRIPT)

Duke steers the car from the driveway as bored Alicia is
in the passenger seat.

                    ALICIA
     Her dog has cancer. I took it to the vet for
     her yesterday.

                    DUKE
     What does that lady do?

                    ALICIA
     Lives off an inheritance. She moved here years
     ago to be an actress. Career never took off.

> DUKE
> Maybe she should try horror movies.

She holds back a giggle. He mimics her. They laugh.

INT. WALTERS' OFFICE RECEPTION - DAY (DUKE'S SCRIPT)

Fish swim around in the huge tank next to the grand piano.

Duke stands as he watches...

Alicia at the counter, where Robin reviews paperwork.

> ROBIN
> Yes, you signed it correctly.

> DUKE
> We can still leave.

Alicia shakes her head.

> ALICIA
> (to Robin)
> Is he here?

> ROBIN
> He will be. Every Monday at eight.

Duke sits. Alicia sits beside him.

> ROBIN
> You'll be so happy. Doctor Walters does
> wonderful work.

Alicia looks to the piano.

> ROBIN
> He was going to be a concert pianist. He chose
> to be a surgeon, instead. Said it's more
> lucrative.

A door opens as smiley, happy nurse in scrubs, KATHY (30),
appears and holds open the door.

> KATHY
> Alicia?

Alicia stands and Duke appears anxious.

> ALICIA
> That'd me be.
> (to Duke)
> Unless your name is Alicia.

He restrains a smile as he nods, "no."

                    KATHY
          (to Duke)
     The designated driver? She'll be ready about
     eleven-thirty.

                    ALICIA
          (winks at Duke)
     See you then, sweetie.

Duke watches as...

Alicia enters the doorway, Kathy follows her in. The door
closes.

Duke sits, thinking.

SURGERY ROOM - LATER (DUKE'S SCRIPT)

Monitors beep.

Alicia's eyes are closed beneath the surgical lights. An
intubation tube in her mouth. Her hair in a surgical cap.

Walters is in medical gloves and scrubs. He places thick,
contact-like guards over Alicia's eyeballs, beneath her
lids.

Kathy hands Walters a scalpel.

                    WALTERS
     Had a good jog on the beach this morning.

He makes an incision in one of Alicia's lower eyelids. As
he pulls the incision open, fatty tissue is exposed.

Kathy adjusts a nob on the monitor.

INT. RECOVERY ROOM - LATER (DUKE'S SCRIPT)

Fine stitches on her upper and lower eyelids Alicia
asleep, propped up in bed. Stitches also hold an incision
closed where the eyelid scar was.

Walters lifts the neck of her gown and gazes at her
breasts. Fondles them. Leans close to her face and lightly
licks her lips. She awakens. He backs away.

                    ALICIA
          (groggy)
     Is?... Wha? What?... What's go --

                    WALTERS
     -- It's okay. You're all done. Simply rest.
     Think good thoughts.

31

                    ALICIA
          It's all so -- Did you? What's...?

She attempts to sit up, he guides her back down.

                    WALTERS
          The anesthesia can play tricks on you. Kathy
          will be here, shortly.

He exits. She slightly opens her eyes. She tries to move
her arms, but sees they are bound to her sides.

I./E. ALICIA'S CAR (MOVING)/CITY - DAY (DUKE'S SCRIPT)

In sunglasses and a baseball cap, Alicia takes deep, slow
breaths in the passenger seat as Duke drives.

                    ALICIA
               (between deep breaths)
          And you say my driving's bad.

                    DUKE
          No worries. I'm just drunk.

                    ALICIA
          Don't. I'm not allowed to laugh.

                    DUKE
          Okay. Just get some beauty rest.

                    ALICIA
          Duke. Seriously. No jokes.

He smirks, as if to joke more. Doesn't. As he drives, he
notices her thoughtfully touch her cheek, then her lips.

                    DUKE
          What's up?

She somberly reclines in the seat.

                    ALICIA
          Drugs are making me feel gross. Or... whatever.

INT. ALICIA'S BEDROOM - LATER (DUKE'S SCRIPT)

Small ice bags cover Alicia's eyes as she's in bed.

                    ALICIA
          I'm paying you for this.

Duke in pajamas, sits beside her.

                    DUKE
          You don't have to.

                    ALICIA
Everyone needs money. Can't tell me you don't.
I've seen your neighborhood.

She takes in and lets out a deep breath.

                    ALICIA
I should go see my brother when I'm healed.

                    DUKE
What does he do up there in the forest?

                    ALICIA
He rakes.

                    DUKE
Rakes?

                    ALICIA
He likes to make lines in the gravel. He can
only do simple things.

                    DUKE
What's wrong with him?

                    ALICIA
Maybe our father hit him too much. He was a
horrible man.

                    DUKE
Do your parents still life there?

                    ALICIA
Both my parents are dead.

The phone rings. She points for him to answer. He gets it.

                    DUKE
          (into phone)
Hello. Alicia's house.

He listens.

                    DUKE
Oh, hi. Yeah, hold on.
          (whispers to Alicia)
Gregory.

He hands over the phone.

                    ALICIA
          (into phone)
Hello... Yeah... That was Duke. You met him on
set -- You're home? already? You said two
weeks...

**INTERCUT PHONE CONV.: GREGORY'S BEACH PATIO/ALICIA'S
BEDROOM**

Gregory with phone to ear as the sun sets over the ocean.

Across the patio, PHIL and NANCY (30s), work a barbecue.

>   **GREGORY**
>   (into phone)
>   Was wondering if you wanted to hang at the
>   beach. The moon'll be full.

>   **ALICIA**
>   I'm a little under the weather.
>   (listens)
>   Just... Female stuff. Cramps.

Duke nearly laughs. She swats his knee.

>   **ALICIA**
>   (into phone)
>   How about next week?

END INTERCUT

>   **GREGORY**
>   (into phone)
>   Next week?! I'm only seventeen miles away. How
>   about tomorrow?

Nancy hands a plate of food to him, he steps inside to...

INT. GREGORY'S APARTMENT - CONT. (DUKE'S SCRIPT)

Gregory, phone to ear, puts the plate of food on the
coffee table as he kicks back on the sofa.

>   **GREGORY**
>   I want to see you... Pretty please.

INT. ALICIA'S BEDROOM - CONT. (DUKE'S SCRIPT)

Blood drips from beneath the ice bag covering Alicia's
eyes.

>   **ALICIA**
>   (into phone)
>   The way you talk.

>   **DUKE**
>   Alicia.

He looks around, reaches for a tissue.

                    ALICIA
              (into phone)
     I want to see you, too. I mean, after this.
     When I feel --

Duke dabs the drop of blood from Alicia's cheek.

                    ALICIA
              (into phone)
     I'm sorry, hold on.

                    DUKE
              (whispers)
     You're bleeding.

She sits up, the ice bags drop, revealing her brutally
bruised and swollen eyes. Blood drips from one eyelid.

                    ALICIA
     What?

She looks in a hand-held mirror. Baffled.

                    ALICIA
              (into phone)
     I'm sorry, I cut my finger. I'll call you
     later... Okay, bye.

She drops the phone. Rushes to the...

BATHROOM

Alicia grabs a tissue, lightly dabs at the bloody eyelid
as she looks in the mirror.

Duke steps in. Winces.

                    ALICIA
     Call that number taped to my phone. It's his
     service number. Then dial my number in and
     nine-one-one.

He rushes out.

Blood drips from her eyelid.

                    ALICIA
     Shit! Why is there still bleeding?

She wipes away more blood.

BEDROOM
Wicked the cat runs as the wireless home phone rings. Duke
picks it up.

                    DUKE
              (looks at phone screen)
          It says unknown caller.

She enters. He hands her the phone. She clicks on.

                    ALICIA
              (into phone)
          Doctor?... Yes, Alicia. There's some
          bleeding... Left eye... Upper.

She looks into the hand-held mirror. More blood drips.

INT. FANCY RESTAURANT - CONT. (DUKE'S SCRIPT)

With cell phone to ear, Dr. Walters, in a sport coat, sits
across from an enhanced young lady (surgically 20s).

                    WALTERS
              (into phone)
          It means you have good vascularization. It'll
          stop. Keep resting sitting up. Keep your head
          above your heart level.

INT. ALICIA'S BEDROOM - CONT. (DUKE'S SCRIPT)

Alicia reclines on the bed.

                    ALICIA
              (into phone)
          Do I keep ice... Okay, light pressure... Yes --
          Okay.

She hangs up. Exhales.

                    ALICIA
          This is bullshit. Why didn't he tell me this
          could happen?

                    DUKE
          Because then you might not have gone through
          with it?

                    ALICIA
          Don't start. It got rid of my scar.

She covers her face. Cries.

He sits on the bed. The phone rings. The answering machine
picks up.

                    ALICIA/ANSWERING MACHINE (V.O.)
          Hello, beautiful person. Leave a message.

INT. STEPHEN'S OFFICE - CONT. (DUKE'S SCRIPT)

Stephen stands frustrated. Picks up his desk phone.

> **STEPHEN**
> (into phone)
> Alicia. Larry Valsa wants to meet with you.
> Call me. Please. A.S.A.P.

He hangs up.

Toby stands in the doorway.

> **STEPHEN**
> What are you looking at?

> **TOBY**
> He's a predator.

> **STEPHEN**
> He wants her for his next film.

> **TOBY**
> Your such a naive *junior agent*. He tries to
> meet every new actress.

Stephen glares at him.

> **STEPHEN**
> What'd you say? You fuckin' bitch.

Toby flashes the bird as he exits. Slams the door.

Stephen angrily stares.

INT. ALICIA'S BEDROOM - MORNING (DUKE'S SCRIPT)

Duke and Wicked the cat sleep near Alicia, who is propped
up, ice bags cover her eyes. Blood streaks both of her
cheeks, onto the pillows.

Duke awakes, looks up to her. Startled.

> **DUKE**
> (whispers)
> Alicia.

> **ALICIA**
> (awakens)
> What?

Feels her cheek, sees blood, bolts to the...

BATHROOM MIRROR

Alicia looks at her bloody eyelids. The sclera are blood red.

> **ALICIA**
> I look like a monster!

BEDROOM

Alicia rushes in, opens a drawer, removes paperwork.

> **ALICIA**
> His phone bill was in the pocket of the jacket he left on set.

She dials the phone.

> **DUKE**
> You said it was your jacket.

She holds the phone to her ear. Then, apparently an answer.

> **ALICIA**
> (into phone)
> There's more bleeding, and the whites of my eyes are blood red.

INTERCUT PHONE CONVERSATION: GOLF COURSE/ALICIA'S BEDROOM

In his golf clothes, Walters stands concerned. Phone to ear.

> **WALTERS**
> (into phone)
> How did you get this number?

Nearby, the pretty young woman touches up her makeup.

> **ALICIA**
> What does that matter?! My eyelids are bleeding!

> **WALTERS**
> You simply need to rest. It's normal to experience some bleeding.

> **ALICIA**
> You didn't tell me this.

Duke lifts the bloody pillow to the bathroom.

> **WALTERS**
> It would be good to drink water.

38

                              ALICIA
             Drink water? It's been four days. You said I'd
             be healed in a week.

                              WALTERS
             Recovery takes time.

                              ALICIA
             Fffffuck you! Drink water? My ass!

Walters holds the phone away from his ear.

                              WALTERS
             Alicia. I deserve more respect than that. I am
             a doctor.

Her hollering can be heard from his phone.

INT. HOSPITAL EXAM ROOM - DAY (DUKE'S SCRIPT)

Duke watches from a chair as...

a DOCTOR types into a computer.

Sunglasses cover Alicia's eyes as she sits on the exam
table.

                              ALICIA
             They burn. And itch.

The Doctor turns to her.

                              DOCTOR
             Let's have a look at those peepers.

Alicia removes the sunglasses from her bruised, swollen
eyes with scabby incisions. The sclera are solid red.

                              DOCTOR
                         (more serious)
             I'll be right back.

The Doctor exits. Duke worriedly looks to Alicia.

                              ALICIA
             Shit. Shit. Shit. FUCK!

INT. SURGERY ROOM - DAY (DUKE'S SCRIPT)

A hand in latex gloves picks up a surgical tool.

Alicia is anesthetized on the table.
A doctor delicately removes stitches from her scabby
eyelids.

A concerned anesthesiologist and a nurse watch.

INT. RESORT HOTEL ROOM - NIGHT (DUKE'S SCRIPT)

Walters stands irritated with the phone to his ear.

> **WALTERS**
> (into phone)
> No. She hasn't made any threats... I haven't
> called the malpractice company. I try to help
> these stupid bitches --
> (listens)
> No. I suggested breast implants, but she
> refused... Fuck!

He kicks the coffee table. It flips.

INT. HOSPITAL ROOM - DAY (DUKE'S SCRIPT)

Gauze bandages cover Alicia's eyes. She's reclined in bed.

> **ALICIA**
> (to self)
> God damn... Fucking... SHIT!

A nurse stops at the doorway. Listens to Alicia.

> **ALICIA**
> I'll fucking kill him. I'll fucking kill that
> fucking bastard. That god damn fucking bastard.

The nurse walks away. Alicia seems to detect the sound.

INT. ALICIA'S LIVING ROOM - DAY (DUKE'S SCRIPT)

Duke sits on the sofa as he pets Wicked the cat.

Alicia, in sunglasses, sits at the desk. Presses a button
on the answering machine.

> **GREGORY/ANSWERING MACHINE (V.O.)**
> Hey, baby. I'm in Mexico working on a
> commercial. Be back in several days. I'd like
> to hear your voice. But, really, I wish you
> were here --

Alicia presses the delete button.

> **PATRICIA/ANSWERING MACHINE (V.O.)**
> (irritating voice)
> This is Patricia Sloan-Bentzine of Sloan-
> Bentzine Public Relations. I don't know if you
> got my previous calls. We need to set press
> junket interviews for your film. Could you

please call? We're talking a possible interview
with Rolling Stone --

Alicia clicks off the answering machine.

> **DUKE**
> Rolling Stone magazine?

> **ALICIA**
> (mundanely)
> All they want are sound bites. Then, they
> distort what you said. And then it's all over
> that Internet thing.

> **DUKE**
> You really do hate the Internet.

She watches him pet the cat.

> **ALICIA**
> I'm sorry, Duke. I really need some time alone.
> I have to think.

He stops petting.

> **DUKE**
> (hesitantly stands)
> Are you... gonna call a lawyer?

> **ALICIA**
> Thanks for everything. We can talk tomorrow.

> **DUKE**
> (grabs motorcycle helmet)
> Okay. Tomorrow... See you.

He gently nudges Wicked with his foot as he exits.

She thoughtfully feels her cheek, then her lips. She
lightly feels a breast, stops, as if calculating the
assault.

INT. STEPHEN'S OFFICE - DAY (DUKE'S SCRIPT)

As he sips a green smoothie, Stephen sits at his desk.

> **STEPHEN**
> (into speaker phone)
> I'm sorry, I don't know where she is.

INTERCUT PHONE CONV.: PATRICIA'S OFFICE/STEPHEN'S OFFICE

At a ridiculously mod desk sits PATRICIA SLOAN-BENTZINE
(50s), dressed for success, nails, brooch, sleek hair.

                    PATRICIA
What about her boyfriend? Is she dating anyone?
Is she gay?

                    STEPHEN
Not that I know of. What would that have to do
with anything? Nobody valid cares.

                    PATRICIA
She's contractually bound to do interviews. She
hasn't done any publicity --

                    STEPHEN
-- She was at Toronto and Sundance.

                    PATRICIA
-- Those were months ago. We need --

                    STEPHEN
-- Patricia. I'm working on it. Okay?

                    PATRICIA
They hired me for film publicity.

                    STEPHEN
          (rolls eyes)
Understood, Patricia. I'll call you when I know
something. Okay?

                    PATRICIA
Please, do. You're her agent, or manager, or
whatever the fuck you are. Get her to
cooperated. It's just as easy for me to put out
bad publicity for her. If she doesn't.

She sneers as she hangs up.

END INTERCUT - STEPHEN'S OFFICE

He hangs up. Sips the green smoothie.

                    STEPHEN
     Okay? Okay? OKAY? Suck my balls. Is she gay.
     Who gives a fuck.

EXT. SIDEWALK CAFE - DAY (FLASHBACK - REAL LIFE)

Alicia and Duke at a table with drinks. Both snack on
pieces of a large muffin. Alicia still has the scar on her
eyelid.

                    DUKE
     My acting coach says I can start auditioning,
     soon.

42

> ALICIA
> Don't wait for anyone to tell you when to start
> living your life.

She watches him eat. He makes a face to humor her, barely
so.

> ALICIA
> People were always telling me what to do. Even
> my husband didn't want me to be an actor.

> DUKE
> You never mentioned you have a husband.

> ALICIA
> I don't. Anymore.

She focuses on and thoughtfully breaks a piece of muffin.

> ALICIA
> It was a bad situation. He was dull. Not
> motivated. At. All. I'm more driven.

He notices...

people in the cafe eye Alicia.

> ALICIA
> I'm not sure if Gregory is ambitious enough for
> me, either.
>   (follows Duke's eyeline)
> What are you...

He keeps an eye on the customers who watch Alicia.

> DUKE
> You really are getting famous.

> ALICIA
>   (notices the customers)
> Must be tourists. Let's leave.

She gets up and walks. He grabs the rest of the muffin.

END FLASHBACK

INT. ALICIA'S LIVING ROOM - DAY (DUKE'S SCRIPT)

Newspapers are scattered on the floor in front of where
disheveled Alicia sits with large sunglasses. Phone to
ear.

                    ALICIA
               (into phone)
     You're the state medical board. You're saying
     you can't stop him from operating on people?

She listens, as she stands, more frustrated.

                    ALICIA
     A complaint form? The police won't arrest him.
     What's wrong with you people? I told you what he
     did -- Have patience? He assaulted me!

She clicks off the phone and fumes as she paces.

INT. GREGORY'S APARTMENT - DAY (DUKE'S SCRIPT)

PHOTOGRAPH: Gregory and Alicia laugh at a party.

Gregory gazes at the photo.

He drops the photo to the coffee table. Stares at it.

INT. DOCTOR WALTERS' OFFICE RECEPTION - DAY (DUKE'S SCRIPT)

Robin watches a well-dressed woman fill out paperwork.

                    ROBIN
               (points)
     Initial there, and sign the back.

Robin puts her hand on the woman's hand.

                    ROBIN
     He does great work. You'll be so happy.

Alicia angrily enters in a baseball cap and sunglasses.

                    ALICIA
     Where is he?

                    ROBIN
     He's not available. Right now.

                    ALICIA
     Do you know where I've been? In the hospital
     for five days. Having infections drained from
     my eyelids, because your boss fucked up, Robin.

                    ROBIN
     I'm so sorry.

                    ALICIA
     Fuck you. Where is he?

The woman grabs her purse and exits.

>   **ROBIN**
>   He's at lunch.

Alicia grabs the piano bench, hurls it at the fish tank.

It shatters. The water splashes to the floor. Fish flip and swirl on the carpet. Alicia exits.

Robin stands shocked. Walters runs in from the back office.

>   **WALTERS**
>   What the hell is --

>   **ROBIN**
>   -- Alicia threw the bench.
>   (reaches for the phone)
>   I'll call the police.

He grabs the phone.

>   **WALTERS**
>   I don't want them involved. Call the building
>   janitor.

He releases the phone. Exits.

Robin watches the fish squirm on the floor. Then dials.

I./E. ALICIA'S CAR (MOVING)/PARKING GARAGE - DAY (DUKE'S SCRIPT)

Alicia drives too fast past the toll kiosk, drives through the lowered arm, it snaps off and flips through the air as she speeds away.

The parking attendant runs from the kiosk out to the street.

INT. LAW OFFICE - DAY (DUKE'S SCRIPT)

Sharply dressed EVAN ZUCKER (50s), sits across from...

livid Alicia in her sunglasses and hat.

>   **ZUCKER**
>   Suing a cosmetic surgeon isn't easy. Especially
>   because -- Let's just say many consider the
>   procedures frivolous, with obvious risks.

She stands, pulls off the sunglasses, her eyelids scarred.

Zucker winces.

                    ALICIA
              (leans toward him)
        You think I can't win a lawsuit?

                    ZUCKER
        I'm not -- There's -- I didn't say that.

She puts on the sunglasses.

He watches as she steps to the window with a view of the
Hollywood sign in the distance.

                    ZUCKER
        It'd help your case if you talk to a
        psychologist. To establish a record of the
        anguish.

                    ALICIA
        I already go to a psychologist.

                    ZUCKER
        Malpractice insurance attorneys do whatever it
        takes to protect the assets of the company.
        You're fighting the insurance company. Not
        really the doctor.

                    ALICIA
        Who protects the patients?

                    ZUCKER
        The State Med Board.

                    ALICIA
        They're useless.

                    ZUCKER
        Doctors don't want to go to court. It becomes
        public record. Malpractice attorneys know an
        actor doesn't want this in the news. They'll
        make it difficult for you.

                    ALICIA
        How?

                    ZUCKER
        Anything to humiliate and discredit you. Dig
        into your past. Question your life choices,
        mental state, job record. Everything is on the
        table. Education. Sexual history. Family
        history. Drug use. Criminal history.

She turns to and stares at him, halted.

                    ZUCKER
        Could there be something...?

She exits. Door slams.

He picks up the phone. Dials.

ZUCKER'S RECEPTION LOBBY - CONT. (DUKE'S SCRIPT)

The ASSISTANT (30s), sees Alicia storm to the elevators.

The Assistant follows Alicia.

> **ASSISTANT**
> Excuse me. I was wondering if I could talk with
> you a second.

Alicia lividly turns to face her.

> **ASSISTANT**
> My friend went to that doctor. When she was
> waking up from surgery, she swears she felt his
> hand on her breast, and he licked her lips.

The elevator doors open. Alicia enters.

> **ASSISTANT**
> She used a different attorney. I have their
> phone number, if you --

> **ALICIA**
> -- He's evil.

The Assistant nervously looks back to the office, then...

> **ASSISTANT**
> (quietly)
> You should know, my boss is friends with Dr.
> Walters. Get a different lawyer.

As Alicia fumes, the elevator doors close.

The Assistant stands at a loss.

ZUCKER'S OFFICE - CONT. (DUKE'S SCRIPT)

Smirky Zucker sits with phone to ear.

> **ZUCKER**
> (into phone)
> Said she found me in the phone book...
> (listens)
> I don't think she'll sue. You're right about
> her tits. She should've let you pump up them
> puppies.

INTERCUT PHONE CONVERSATION: WALTERS' OFFICE/ZUCKER'S OFFICE

Walters reclines in his chair, the phone to his ear.

> **WALTERS**
> (snickers)
> Let the record state.

> **ZUCKER**
> She seemed triggered when I mentioned lawsuits could dig into criminal history. What do you know about her past?

E./I. CITY STREET/ALICIA'S CAR (MOVING) - DAY (DUKE'S SCRIPT)

Furious Alicia speeds dangerously in and around traffic.

She stops too fast at a red light. She looks up to see...

BILLBOARD LOOMING OVER INTERSECTION: A woman's airbrushed face, "Enhance your beauty. Call Lotus Cosmetic Surgery, Today!"

Alicia seethes as she looks at the billboard.

> **STEPHEN (O.S.)**
> Alicia!

She notices in the...

black convertible next to her is Stephen at the wheel.

> **STEPHEN**
> Why won't you call me?

Alicia speeds through the red light. Screeches to a halt to avoid...

a stunned pedestrian halted in the crosswalk.

Alicia's sunglasses fall off.

> **ALICIA**
> Fuck!

She brushes hair from her face, sees the...

pedestrian who winces at the site of Alicia.

Alicia replaces the sunglasses and speeds away.

> **STEPHEN'S CAR**
> He sits with mouth agape.

                        STEPHEN
      What. The. Fuck?

INT. DR. LINDER'S OFFICE - DAY (DUKE'S SCRIPT)

Linder patiently sits in the analyst chair.

                        LINDER
      Alicia?

Alicia wears big sunglasses as she reclines on the sofa.

                        LINDER
      Are you thinking of hurting someone?

                        ALICIA
      Thinking and doing are two different things.

                        LINDER
      You know this is your safe space.

                        ALICIA
      Nothing's really safe. We're all in constant
      danger. It captures some people, while others
      live in bliss.

Linder considers her, as if unsurely.

**INT. COFFEE HOUSE - DAY (REAL LIFE MIXED WITH DUKE'S
SCRIPT)**

A large, framed drawing of Edgar Allen Poe peers down
onto...

people at tables, some with laptops. Among them...

Duke, who types on a laptop.

His girlfriend Jennifer from the opening scene sits with
him as she reads a book. Across from them sits...

Alicia, morose in sunglasses and a hat, as if tragically
alone. (She's not there, but is in Duke's imagination.)

                        JENNIFER
      How far are you with the script?

                        DUKE
           (as he types)
      Nearly halfway done.

Jennifer watches as...

Duke watches...
Alicia watch the...

CASH REGISTER COUNTER: A burly guy with long blond hair pays for a coffee.

Duke thoughtfully gazes at Alicia as he types.

> **JENNIFER**
> Inspiration incoming.

Alicia stares at the blond guy.

Duke watches her as he types his thoughts of this...

INT. RAMSHACKLE HOUSE - NIGHT (FLASHBACK - DUKE'S SCRIPT)

In T-shirt and cutoffs, Alicia sits on the floor against the antique stove of the cluttered kitchen.

Seated at the table, a half-naked, ruggedly handsome man with long blond hair, DALE (40s), finishes dinner.

> **DALE**
> Acting? That's bullshit.

> **ALICIA**
> We can move to Los Angeles.

> **DALE**
> Not moving to that shit hole city.

> **ALICIA**
> I had a dream I was a movie star.

He stands. Opens the fridge. Grabs a beer.

> **DALE**
> You also dream that you drive in the ocean. Gonna do that, too? Enough of this actress bullshit.

He swigs the beer.

> **ALICIA**
> What am I supposed to be doing?

> **DALE**
> (turns to leave)
> How about shut the fuck up.

She rises, grabs a pan from the sink. Throws.

It hits his shoulder.

> **DALE**
> (marches toward her)
> God damn.

She attacks him. Things fall, shatter. He fends her off. Wrestles her to the floor. Pins her down. Her eyelid bleeds from a cut (where the scar forms).

> **DALE**
> (angrily)
> You finished?

He holds her down as they catch their breath. He lets go, stands. He takes another beer from the fridge. Opens it.

> **DALE**
> You wouldn't want to live away from your weirdo brother, anyway.

He takes a swig from the beer. Swaggers from the room.

Her eyelid bleeds as she sits up against a cabinet.

> **ALICIA**
> Fuck you. He's an innocent angel.

She wipes her face. Sees blood on her hand.

END FLASHBACK

INT. COFFEE HOUSE - DAY (REAL LIFE MIXED WITH DUKE'S SCRIPT)

Duke's imaginary Alicia watches the Blond Man at the counter. He takes his coffee.

> **BLOND MAN**
> (as he passes Alicia)
> How you doin?

Alicia considers him as he confidently swaggers to the exit.

> **DUKE**
> See something you like?

Jennifer looks up from her book.

> **JENNIFER**
> What?

> **DUKE**
> Nothing. Just thinking.

Jennifer continues to read the book as Alicia rises and walks away.

Duke types as he watches. His thoughts are of...

EXT. COFFEE HOUSE - DAY (DUKE'S SCRIPT)

Alicia exits and looks around. A random car skids onto the sidewalk, nearly hits her, smashes into a wall. Alicia stands still, as if in shock. She drops her coffee.

People run over to help the driver in the car.

The Blond Man touches Alicia's arm.

> **BLOND MAN**
> You okay?

Duke exits the coffee house in different clothes than he had on inside the coffee house. He sees...

Alicia gets in her car. Starts the engine, speeds away.

> **BLOND MAN**
> (to Duke)
> Hey, bud, isn't she an actress?

Duke ignores him as he watches Alicia's car speed away.

Random pedestrians help the accident driver.

INT. ALICIA'S LIVING ROOM - DAY (DUKE'S SCRIPT)

Wicked the cat is on the desk being petted by Alicia, who is in sunglasses.

> **STEPHEN/ANSWERING MACHINE (V.O.)**
> Alicia, why wouldn't you talk to me? You nearly crashed your car. Please, help me understand --

Alicia presses the delete button.

> **GREGORY/ANSWERING MACHINE (V.O.)**
> I'm back in town. Would really like to see you. Call me. Or, just come over --

Alicia presses the delete button.

> **PATRICIA/ANSWERING MACHINE (V.O.)**
> Alicia, it's Patricia. The press junket is tomorrow. The producers are freaking out. Please call --

Alicia presses the machine off. She notices...

the door curtains have shadows of two people outside.

OUTSIDE THE DOOR

Sharply dressed Stephen and prim Patricia step to the door. Stephen wipes his nose, looks at his fingers.

> **STEPHEN**
> Is there any cocaine on my nostrils?

> **PATRICIA**
> (gives a lookover)
> No. Why don't you simply smoke weed?

> **STEPHEN**
> Pot makes people lazy and dumb.

He knocks on the door.

> **STEPHEN**
> Her car is here. She's here.

INSIDE

Alicia looks through a small crack in the curtains.

> **STEPHEN (O.S.)**
> Alicia? Larry Valsa wants you for his film. This is what we worked for, babe. C'mon, open the door.

OUTSIDE

Stephen and Patricia wait.

> **STEPHEN**
> (whispers to Patricia)
> It's so unprofessional. We can't even find anyone who knows her.

> **PATRICIA**
> (whispers)
> Maybe she's a drug addict.

> **STEPHEN**
> That'd be my fucking luck.

Patricia uses her French-tipped nails to tap the door.

> **PATRICIA**
> Alicia, it's Patricia. Let's do lunch, honey. Are you in there?

INSIDE

Alicia watches as the shadows on the curtain move away. As the voices fade, she peeks through the curtains.

OUTSIDE

Stephen and Patricia stand nearly appalled before...

freakish Isabella with her sickly, rigid dog, Happy.

> **ISABELLA**
> A manager? I'm an actress, too. I'm currently
> seeking representation.

Patricia takes Stephen's arm, leads him down the driveway.

Isabella appears perplexed by the dismissal.

INSIDE

Alicia sits and rests her head on the desk.

EXT. HOLLYWOOD BLVD. NEWS STAND - NIGHT (DUKE'S SCRIPT)

Magazine pages are flipped through. Stops at an ad for
Alicia's forthcoming film "Driven," with her image
prominent.

Alicia in hat and sunglasses, closes the magazine.

The newsstand worker is busy with a customer.

Alicia shoves the magazine into her purse. Looks to the...

NEIGHBORING PORN STORE

Next to the door stands a tattooed, muscular man with
facial piercings and dressed in leather. He smokes a
cigarette. The door is painted in big words: "The
Dungeon."

INT. THE DUNGEON - DAY - CONT. (DUKE'S SCRIPT)

At the register, a tattooed woman reads a porn magazine.

Alicia browses the sex toys, straps, whips. She notices...

a shirtless, tattooed man tries on a studded leather vest.

Alicia is nearly bumped into by a grim muscular man who
makes his way to his friend trying on the vest.

Alicia runs her hand over a rubber bondage outfit with a
head covering that has eye and nostril openings, and a
zippered mouth. She sticks her fingers into the eye
openings.

INT. ALICIA'S LIVING ROOM - NIGHT (DUKE'S SCRIPT)

Duke relaxes on the floor near the sofa where Alicia reclines in sunglasses and pajamas. A plate of food sits next to her.

> ALICIA
> Duke, I'm not a person to be looked up to.

> DUKE
> Why are you saying this?

She looks at a fork full of food.

> DUKE
> Did you call the new doctor?

> ALICIA
> I've seen three damn doctors.

> DUKE
> What'd they say?

She tiredly picks a lettuce leaf from the salad. Holds it up to the side table lamp.

LEAF: The veiny patterns are illuminated.

> ALICIA
> So many patterns in everything. Patterns in life. It's all patterns. Networks. Tied together.

> DUKE
> Why won't you eat?

He tiredly leans his head on the sofa. His eyes close. She puts down the leaf and massages his scalp as he relaxes.

> ALICIA
> Thank you for being here.

INT./EXT. WALTERS' BEDROOM/BALCONY - NIGHT (DUKE'S SCRIPT)

A young, pretty woman cries as she gets dressed.

Walters stands faced away at the balcony doors as he stares out at the dark ocean.

> WALTERS
> Take the cash on the table. Not that you were good enough for it. Who taught you how to fuck?

She wipes her tears, grabs her purse, takes the cash. Exits.

INT. ALICIA'S LIVING ROOM - NIGHT (DUKE'S SCRIPT)

Duke awakens on the floor. Sits up.

Alicia is asleep on the sofa, still in her sunglasses. Wicked sleeps next to her.

He picks up his motorcycle helmet, quietly exits.

BATHROOM SHOWER - DAY

Steamy water streams over Alicia's hair, which hides her face as she hugs her knees where she sits, still in her pajamas on the shower floor.

LIVING ROOM WINDOW

The curtains flutter at the open window. Outside, Weird Isabella is in the yard with her decrepit dog. Isabella glances back and forth from the dog to the window.

DESK

The pages of a phone book flip in the breeze.

ON THE PAGES: Cosmetic surgeon ads feature vibrant models with idealized faces and big breasts.

On the floor, cut into pieces are headshot photos of Alicia.

A washcloth over her face, Alicia lies on the floor dressed in a robe. She stops breathing. Her jaw relaxes. She feels the pulse of her neck. Puts a knife blade to it.

The landline phone rings. The answering machine picks up.

> **ALICIA/ANSWERING MACHINE (V.O.)**
> Hello, beautiful person. Leave a message.

> **STEPHEN/ANSWERING MACHINE (V.O.)**
> Alicia. Pick up. Pick up the damn phone! Larry Valsa needs an answer. You don't have to audition. The studio people are not happy. Call me. Or, I'm no longer your manager.

She curls into a fetal position.

INT. GROCERY MARKET CHECKOUT LINE - DAY (DUKE'S SCRIPT)

Duke pays for groceries. Gregory walks past. Stops and turns as he notices Duke.

> **GREGORY**
> Wayne?

Duke stops as he recognizes Gregory.

> **DUKE**
> Oh... Hey, Gregory. My name's Duke.

> **GREGORY**
> Oh, sorry. Right. You're Alicia's friend.
> How're you doin?

Duke gathers the grocery bags. Gregory waits.

> **DUKE**
> Okay. Just getting some food.

> **GREGORY**
> Do you know if she's in town?

> **DUKE**
> Alicia? Yeah. She's in town.

> **GREGORY**
> Is she okay? She was sick.

Duke fidgets with the grocery bags.

> **DUKE**
> No -- I mean. Not sick. Or, that I know of.

Gregory takes out his wallet, hands Duke a business card.

> **GREGORY**
> If you talk with her, could you tell her to
> give me a call?

> **DUKE**
> Yeah, sure.

> **GREGORY**
> Cool. Hope you're doing good.
>   (pats Duke's shoulder)
> Hope to see you on a set, soon.

Gregory heads deeper into the store. Duke exits.

EXT. ALICIA'S FRONT STEPS - DAY (DUKE'S SCRIPT)

Duke appears worried as he holds groceries.

The door partially opens. Through the crack, barely seen
is Alicia in sunglasses, hair a mess.

Duke steps to enter, but she keeps the door nearly shut.

                    ALICIA
        Sorry, Duke. You can leave the bags on the
        step.

She holds out the cash. He lowers the bags, takes the
money.

                    DUKE
        Gregory wants to talk with you.

                    ALICIA
        Why would you say that?

                    DUKE
        I saw him at the store. He asked me to tell you
        to call him.

                    ALICIA
        Thanks, Duke. I'm sorry.

She closes the door. He waits. Unsurely, he puts the money
in his pocket.

INT. ISABELLA'S LIVING ROOM - CONT. (DUKE'S SCRIPT)

Isabella holds her ratty dog as she peeks through the
curtains to see Duke's car pull from the driveway.

INT. ALICIA'S BEDROOM - NIGHT (DUKE'S SCRIPT)

Alicia, a mess in sunglasses and robe as she digs through
the pockets of Walters' jacket she stole. Pulls out
papers. Drops the jacket. Pauses to read.

                    ALICIA
                (to self)
        Santa Monica beach. Morning jogs.

LIVING ROOM - LATER - NIGHT (DUKE'S SCRIPT)

The cat sits on the sofa watching...

Alicia pace in sunglasses and robe. She looks to the...

DIGITAL CLOCK: "3:40 A.M."

INT. ALICIA'S DINING ROOM - DAY (DUKE'S SCRIPT)

Alicia relaxes her head on the table. Half dressed. A
knock at the door. She lifts her head.

OUTSIDE THE DOOR

Gregory holds flowers as he waits.

INT. DUKE'S APARTMENT - DAY (REAL LIFE)

Printed script pages and screenwriting books are scattered
on the desk where Duke sits, the laptop in front of him.
He speaks as if he might be on a speaker phone (he's not).

>   DUKE
>   Why didn't you open the door?

**INTERCUT PHONE CONVERSATION: ALICIA'S LIVING ROOM/DUKE'S
APT. (REAL LIFE MIXED WITH DUKE'S SCRIPT)**

Alicia, on the phone and in her sunglasses smells the
flowers she places in a vase.

>   ALICIA
>   (into phone)
>   I don't want him to see me.

Duke picks up a script page, seems to read aloud from it,
as if maybe talking to a speaker phone.

>   DUKE
>   Maybe you should call him.

Alicia picks up trash from the floor.

Duke appears to read from his computer screen.

>   DUKE
>   At least call, and thank him for the flowers.

He types.

ALICIA'S KITCHEN - CONT. (DUKE'S SCRIPT)

Alicia remains on the phone as she enters the messy room.

>   ALICIA
>   (into phone)
>   Not everything has a meaning, Duke.

She picks up a roach from the counter. Looks at it as it
wiggles. She drops it into the sink. Turns on the water.

The roach struggles against the flow of water in the sink.

>   ALICIA
>   I have to go. We'll talk, later... Okay... Bye.

She hangs up. Turns on the sink's garbage disposal.

EXT. SANTA MONICA BEACH - SUNSET (REAL LIFE)

The ocean reflects the tangerine sky as if the water is on fire. Faint sounds of piano music are heard.

BEACH BIKE TRAIL/WALTERS' HOUSE - CONT. (REAL LIFE MIXED WITH DUKE'S SCRIPT)

Duke skates on Rollerblades with Jennifer. He slows to a stop, as he hears the piano music.

Jennifer stops to see Duke look behind him as he watches...

Alicia (in Duke's imagination), in sunglasses slowly skates as she looks at the mini mansions along the bike trail with the cliffs in the background. She stops. The piano music continues.

Duke watches...

Alicia as she eyes Walters' house.

INT. WALTERS' LIVING ROOM - CONT. (REAL LIFE)

Walters, in a bathrobe, plays a piano near a wall of open glass doors overlooking the beach bike trail where Jennifer watches Duke as he watches Alicia gazing at Walter's house.

BIKE TRAIL - CONT. (DUKE'S SCRIPT MIXED WITH REAL LIFE)

Alicia remains is stopped on her skates as she watches...

Walters' house. The piano music continues as Walters can be seen inside at the piano.

Duke watches as Jennifer waits.

> **JENNIFER**
> (to Duke)
> What's going on?

Jennifer wipes sweat from her brow as she watches Duke. His thoughts are of...

INT. BEVERLY HILLS MANSION - NIGHT (DUKE'S SCRIPT)

A wine glass is filled by a butler for a Botoxed woman.

Fingers dance across grand piano keys playing elegant music. It's Walters, dressed in a sharp suit.

Suited wealthy men and their cosmetic doll wives watch.

A DAPPER MAN (60s), is next to his TROPHY WIFE (30s).

Walters pauses from the piano. He pulls out his cell phone. Looks at the screen. Displeasure traces his face.

> **WALTERS**
> (to guests)
> I'm sorry. I must take this.

> **TROPHY WIFE**
> Oh, please continue, Bernard.

> **DAPPER MAN**
> I bet all the ladies say that.

Pacifying laughter among the guests.

> **WALTERS**
> (stands)
> Excuse me a moment.

The guests converse.

HALLWAY

Walters with phone to his ear.

> **WALTERS**
> (into phone)
> Why are you calling me?... I can't -- What?

INTERCUT: ALICIA'S LIVING ROOM/MANSION (DUKE'S SCRIPT)

Alicia in sunglasses, phone to ear. The room a mess.

> **ALICIA**
> (into phone)
> Your house on the beach. With the piano. I'll call you there.

> **WALTERS**
> Are you spying on me? Don't call. I'm going home to bed. I have to get up early --

> **ALICIA**
> -- For surgery?! You gonna fuck up someone else, Walter?

Walters nervously looks down the hall. All clear.

> **ALICIA**
> Someone should slice your face into pieces, you fucking asshole!

END INTERCUT

Walters clicks off the phone, places it in his suit coat as he reenters the dinner party. Puts on his pleasant face.

ALICIA'S LIVING ROOM (DUKE'S SCRIPT)

She's red with anger.

> **ALICIA**
> (into phone)
> I haven't slept in weeks. Do you sleep?

As she realizes he has hung up, she seethes in anger.

INT. KICKBOXING CLASS - DAY (DUKE'S SCRIPT)

Rows of gym members attack punching bags as pop music blares.

Alicia in sunglasses and baseball cap attacks a punching bag.

The instructor stops to watch Alicia.

A few class members notice as...

Alicia furiously attacks the bag, as if to kill.

EXT. SANTA MONICA - PALISADES PARK - DAY (DUKE'S SCRIPT)

Strollers and joggers pass along the dirt pathway.

At the concrete fence along the edge of the cliff, Alicia looks through the binoculars down below to...

SANTA MONICA BEACH MANSIONS/PACIFIC COAST HIGHWAY (P.C.H.)

On the back side of Walters' house, the garage door opens.

PALISADES PARK

A nosy park stroller sees Alicia. The stroller stops at the fence to look over the cliff to the houses below.

Alicia with binoculars continues to watch down below...

WALTERS' DRIVEWAY/P.C.H.

Walters in his Mercedes pulls onto the highway as the garage door closes. He speeds away, in southbound traffic.

PALISADES PARK

Alicia in sunglasses watches the P.C.H. traffic.

INT. MEDICAL OFFICE PATIENT ROOM - DAY (DUKE'S SCRIPT)

A doctor examines Alicia's eyelids. Done with the exam, Alicia puts on her sunglasses. As...
the doctor makes notes in a file.

Alicia looks to see...

her distorted reflection in the steel paper towel dispenser.

She looks back at the doctor who continues to write notes.

EXT. MELROSE SIDEWALK CAFE - DAY (DUKE'S SCRIPT)

Duke wolfs down a chunk of sandwich.

Alicia is in sunglasses and hat. Lazily picks at her food.

                    ALICIA
          Referred me to a doctor who works with burn
          victims... How lovely. Another doctor
          appointment.

                    DUKE
          Can he do what you need?

                    ALICIA
          Seems to think that it isn't very difficult to
          fix.

A WAITRESS approaches.

                    WAITRESS
          How is everything?

                    ALICIA
          You don't wanna know.

The waitress becomes concerned.

                    ALICIA
          The food's fine. Thank you.

                    WAITRESS
               (relieved)
          Aren't you in that Sharon Grock film that's
          coming out? My boyfriend edited the commercials
          for it. That's you, right?

Duke smiles as Alicia glumly looks back at him.

                    WAITRESS
          I'm sorry. Maybe I shouldn't have intruded.

                              DUKE
          I told her she should get used to being
          recognized.

Duke attempts to edge Alicia on with a smile.
Doesn't work.

                            WAITRESS
          Let me know if you'd like any desserts. On the
          house.

The Waitress goes to the next customer. Duke takes a big
bite of his sandwich. Jokingly eats with his mouth open.

Alicia takes a piece of bread and playfully tosses it at
him. He catches it and shoves it into his packed mouth.
She nearly giggles. He nearly chokes.

She finally laughs.

INT. EXAM ROOM - DAY (DUKE'S SCRIPT)

DOCTOR REYNOLDS (60s), writes in a chart.

Sad Alicia sits wearing sunglasses.

                            REYNOLDS
          They need to heal for at least several more
          months. The blood vessels need time to
          reconnect. The scar tissues need to relax.

                             ALICIA
          Will they look normal?

He leans up against the counter. Thinks.

                            REYNOLDS
          It may take a second surgery... But there
          should be significant improvement.

                             ALICIA
          Years. Then... and... maybe.

                            REYNOLDS
          For the best results, it's not something to be
          rushed. Healing takes time.

She sadly nods.

                            REYNOLDS
          I've heard of Walters being a medical
          consultant on movie sets. Another of his
          patients was here years ago. But... not this
          bad.

                    ALICIA
        He's done this to other people?

                    REYNOLDS
        For now, you need to heal... I'd like to see
        you in three months.

She seems to have disconnected. He waits.

                    REYNOLDS
        Can we do that?

                    ALICIA
            (finally)
        I guess I'll have to.

LOBBY

A reserved office manager, CARLA, sits at a computer.

Alicia in her sunglasses stands at the counter.

                    CARLA
        Be sure to give us a call if there are any
        changes.

Carla hands Alicia a reservation card.

                    CARLA
        I think you chose the right doctor. He does
        amazing work.

Alicia forces a blink of a smile.

INT. DUKE'S LIVING ROOM - DAY (DUKE'S SCRIPT)

Duke sits at the laptop, with phone to his ear.

                    DUKE
            (into phone)
        Maybe it'll heal faster than that.

INTERCUT PHONE CONVERSATION: ALICIA'S BEDROOM/DUKE'S APT.

Tangled in blankets, Alicia is on the phone.

                    ALICIA
            (into phone)
        Gregory stopped calling.

                    DUKE
        Call him. He said he wanted you to.

Wicked snuggles up to Alicia and purrs.

                    DUKE
          Are you there?

                    ALICIA
          I'm gonna take a nap. Call me when you get home
          from acting class.

She hangs up and thoughtfully pets the cat.

                    ALICIA
               (to the cat)
          What would happen to you if I left?

The cat purrs as Alicia pets him.

INT. DUKE'S APARTMENT - NIGHT (REAL LIFE)

Jennifer massages Duke's shoulders. He is in different
clothes than the previous scene and sits at the table. He
stares at the laptop screen. A thought clicks. He types...

EXT. HOLLYWOOD GAS STATION - DAY (DUKE'S SCRIPT)

The gas pump display adds up the gallons.

Alicia, in sunglasses, gasses up her car. She notices...

ON THE STREET

A city bus stops. On its side is a large movie poster of
"Driven" that features Alicia's face. A rider exits the
bus.

GAS STATION

Alicia watches.

                    ALICIA
               (to self)
          Holy. Fucking shit.

ACROSS STREET - LIQUOR STORE

As the bus pulls away, Walters exits the store and gets
into his Mercedes.

GAS STATION

Panicky, Alicia quickly returns the pump nozzle. Jumps in.
Door slams. Starts the car. Speeds away.

**E./I. WALTERS'/ALICIA'S CARS (MOVING)/HOLLYWOOD - CONT.
(DUKE'S SCRIPT)**

Walters' Mercedes is followed by Alicia's car.

She zooms around him, pulls in front of him. Slams on the brakes.

Walters skids to a stop. Waits. Irritated. Pulls around her and speeds off.

CORNER OF STREET BY STOP SIGN

Alicia speeds up next to Walters' stopped car.

He looks to see her roll down her window.

He speeds through the intersection, nearly hits a car.

She speeds ahead of him and cuts him off.

His car nearly runs over a ravaged HOMELESS WOMAN, and...

smashes into a fence and straddles a low brick wall.

The ravaged HOMELESS WOMAN laughs outrageously.

Alicia gets out of her car. Approaches Walters' car.

> **WALTERS**
> (rolls down window)
> You insane bitch!

He rolls up his window as she kicks it.

> **ALICIA**
> Now you're a psychiatrist?

She picks up a brick and smashes his windshield.

> **HOMELESS WOMAN**
> (hollers)
> You get him, sister!

Alicia gets into her car. Speeds away.

Walters opens his car door. Dials his phone.

INTERCUT PHONE CONV.: ZUCKER'S OFFICE/WALTERS' CAR (DUKE'S SCRIPT)

Zucker sits back in his chair, phone to ear.

> **ZUCKER**
> (into phone)
> Shattered your windshield?

Walters with phone to ear considers the damaged car.

                         WALTERS
                     (into phone)
          I'll say I was distracted. A homeless person
          ran across the street. Whatever.

The Homeless Woman passes by and spits on the car.

                    HOMELESS WOMAN
                      (hollers)
          Bastard! All you men are bastards! Every damn
          one of you! Fuckheads!

Walters watches her meander away.

EXT. GREGORY'S BEACH PATIO - DAY (DUKE'S SCRIPT)

Gregory with phone to ear, stares out at the ocean.

INTERCUT PHONE CONVERSATION: DUKE'S APT./GREGORY'S PATIO

Duke with phone to ear, looks at Gregory's business card.

                        DUKE
                     (into phone)
          Just wondering if you called her.

                       GREGORY
          Duke. Listen. Is there something going on that
          I should know about?

Duke fidgets with the card.

                        DUKE
          Her movie's coming out.

                       GREGORY
          Yeah, I kind of know that. Her movie posters
          are all over town. Did she tell you to call me?

                        DUKE
          No.

                       GREGORY
          What's going on here, Duke?

                        DUKE
          She likes you. I think she's lonely. I'm sorry.
          I have to go.

                       GREGORY
          Duke, what the fuck?

                        DUKE
          I'm sorry.

Duke hangs up.

END INTERCUT - GREGORY'S PATIO

Baffled, Gregory stares at his phone.

EXT. ISABELLA'S BACK DOORSTEP - DAY (DUKE'S SCRIPT)

Isabella, mascara smeared by tears, cradles her decrepit dog, Happy, in a blanket.

Alicia in sunglasses and hat, gently takes the dog.

> **ALICIA**
> It's the right thing to do.

Isabella cries. Turns and enters her house. The door slams. Her cries louden.

Alicia carries Happy to her car.

INT. ANIMAL VET EXAM ROOM - LATER - DAY (DUKE'S SCRIPT)

A VET (60s) fills a syringe from a tiny injectable bottle.

Alicia in her sunglasses and hat, pets Happy, still wrapped in a blanket on the table.

> **VET**
> This is rather fast.

> **ALICIA**
> How do you know it's enough?

> **VET**
> It'll be more than enough... Are you okay with this?

> **ALICIA**
> (pets Happy one last time)
> I think I'd rather step out.

She pauses at the doorway.

> **ALICIA**
> You can go ahead with it.

HALLWAY

Alicia steps from the room. Glances back to see...

the Vet is busy with the injection.

SUPPLY ROOM

Alicia slips into the room, sees a cabinet with an open padlock. Opens it. Takes several of the small injectable bottles of anesthetic. She slips them into her purse.

EXT. ALICIA'S GUEST HOUSE - DAY (DUKE'S SCRIPT)

Gregory knocks on the door.

Wicked the cat pokes through the curtains inside the window.

>   GREGORY
> Hey, little kitty. Is Alicia home?

INT. ISABELLA'S HOUSE - CONT. (DUKE'S SCRIPT)

A ray of sunlight streams onto Isabella's face, makeup streaked from tears. She peeks through the curtains.

INT. ALICIA'S LIVING ROOM - CONT. (DUKE'S SCRIPT)

Alicia, in sunglasses and pajamas listens near the door.

OUTSIDE

Gregory hesitantly walks away. A noise at the door. He turns.

The door opens just a sliver.

>   ALICIA
> I'm sorry, Gregory.

He squints to see her.

>   GREGORY
> Are you okay?

A glance of Alicia in sunglasses.

ISABELLA'S LIVING ROOM

Isabella watches through the curtains.

>   GREGORY (O.S.)
> Alicia, what's going on?

OUTSIDE

Gregory waits.

>   ALICIA
> Something happened.

                    GREGORY
          What happened?

He approaches the door.

                    ALICIA
              (nearly closes the door)
          No.

She opens it a sliver.

                    ALICIA
          Maybe things come full circle.

                    GREGORY
          What do you mean?

The door remains cracked open.

                    GREGORY
          Can we go for a walk?

                    ALICIA
          I'm sorry... I liked you.

She closes the door.

                    GREGORY
          Come on. What's going on? I'm trying, Alicia.
          Talk with me.

He looks around. Waits. Frustratedly walks away.

INT. GREGORY'S APARTMENT - NIGHT (DUKE'S SCRIPT)

TV SCREEN: A sports game is paused.

Phil sits on the sofa. Gregory stands nearby.

                    PHIL
          You're too nice. Ignore her. She'll come
          running back for attention. It's what women
          do. Play games.

                    GREGORY
          What a concept.

                    PHIL
          It's true, man. Assholes always have chicks.
          Nice guys don't. You're too nice.

Phil flicks through TV stations.

Alicia's face is briefly on one of the stations.

                    GREGORY
Wait! Go back!

                    PHIL
What?

                    GREGORY
Click back two stations.

Phil presses the remote.

TV SCREEN: The last moment of a clip shows Alicia's new
film "Driven," then two FILM REVIEWERS talk.

                FILM REVIEWER 1
This is film is quiet twisted, as can be
expected from director Sharon Grock.

                FILM REVIEWER 2
The lead actress, Alicia Dover, proves herself
worthy. This is her breakthrough role. We tried
to land an interview, but her people say she's
busy on a new project.

                FILM REVIEWER 1
A powerful performance. She'll likely be one
busy actress, after this film. In other movie
news...

                    GREGORY
Bullshit!

Phil dismissively flicks to a sports channel.

Gregory stares.

INT. STEPHEN'S OFFICE - DAY (DUKE'S SCRIPT)

Stephen fiddles to get his folded shirt sleeves at the
same length. Frustrated, he unfolds one to fold it again.

Toby enters with a cup of coffee. Places it in on the
desk.

                    TOBY
I saw Alicia.

                    STEPHEN
Where?!

                    TOBY
She like was like, in front of like, the like
coffee house?

                    STEPHEN
And?... Did you talk with her?

                    TOBY
Like. No? It would like have been like
difficult to like talk with her?

                    STEPHEN
Why?

                    TOBY
She was like in like a movie poster like on the
side of like... a bus?

Toby giggles and heads for the door. The coffee cup misses
Toby, splatters against a wall. Toby turns to him.

                    STEPHEN
Do you think this is a joke, Toby?!

                    TOBY
Calm the fuck down.

                    STEPHEN
Calm down?!

                    TOBY
Stop the cocaine. Find other actors to
represent. You have seven clients. And obsess
over one.

                    STEPHEN
I worked damn hard to get her career to where
it is.

                    TOBY
Pffft.

Toby exits.

                    STEPHEN
Asshole!

EXT. BEACH/WALTERS' HOUSE - NIGHT (DUKE'S SCRIPT)

Piano music is heard as Alicia sits in the sand facing
away from the water. She watches...

WALTERS' HOUSE: Through the large open glass doors,
Walters is seen at the piano as he plays it.

Alicia continues to watch.

INT. ALICIA'S LIVING ROOM - NIGHT (DUKE'S SCRIPT)

The table is scattered with the little rubber-topped injectable bottles Alicia stole from the animal hospital.

She uses a magnifying glass to read the label of a bottle.

BEDROOM - LATER

Ravey sitar dance music plays in the dimly-lit room, Alicia sits on the bed as she slowly injects a needle into a vein. Removes the needle.

She reclines onto pillows.

LIVING ROOM - LATER

In the dimly-lit and messy room. Drugged-out Alicia mildly dances to the sitar music.

BEDROOM - MORNING

Wicked sprawled out next to sleeping Alicia. The cat wags her tail against Alicia's cheek. Alicia's eyes slightly open.

BEDROOM - NIGHT

Duke in pajamas watches as...

Alicia is in sunglasses. She kicks clutter away from the closet door. Digs through clothes.

She tosses clothes into an open suitcase.

> **DUKE**
> You're gonna stay until your doctor appointment? Three months from now?

> **ALICIA**
> That's one thought.

She tosses socks into the suitcase.

> **ALICIA**
> (zips the suitcases)
> Thoughts. Words. Sounds. Dreams. Memories. Feelings. They're just a bunch of chemical interactions.

> **DUKE**
> I don't know what you mean.

She places a black plastic bag featuring the logo "The Dungeon" in one suitcase. Closes it.

                    DUKE
    What's that?

                    ALICIA
    A new raincoat.

His eyes don't believe.

She closes the other suitcase, and lounges on the bed.

                    ALICIA
    The other day, I cut him off in traffic. He
    smashed into a brick wall. Then, I smashed his
    windshield. You should have seen the look on
    his face.

                    DUKE
    The doctor?

She removes her sunglasses and puts on a dark sleeping
mask as she rests back onto pillows.

                    DUKE
    What?... Did the police come?

                    ALICIA
    He won't call the police.

                    DUKE
    Why?

She pulls the covers over her.

                    DUKE
    Why?... What if he did? And, they come here to
    get you?

                    ALICIA
    He won't call the police.

                    DUKE
    Is that why you're going away, so the cops
    can't find you?

                    ALICIA
    No.

                    DUKE
    What're you gonna do up there?

He watches her.

                    DUKE
    I don't want you to leave. You're my only
    friend.

                    ALICIA
Duke.

                    DUKE
What?

                    ALICIA
Don't be afraid of your love.

Wicked jumps up onto the bed and settles next to her.

Duke saddens as he watches Alicia fall to sleep.

INT. STEPHEN'S OFFICE - NIGHT (DUKE'S SCRIPT)

Stephen at the desk watches...

a line of cocaine is snorted by Patricia.

                    STEPHEN
          What if we got a photo double. She can wear big
          sunglasses and a hat, like in the movie. We can
          tell her what to say in the interviews.

                    PATRICIA
          What are you, high?

                    STEPHEN
          No. Ew. I don't smoke weed!

They drug laugh.

                    PATRICIA
          Don't you know anything about her family? -- Or
          -- Wait! What if she's in a mental hospital?

                    STEPHEN
          Isn't that what this is? She'd be here now.

                    PATRICIA
          Be here, now. Like Ram Dass.

Drugged-out laughter. Stephen preps a line of cocaine.

                    PATRICIA
          Seriously. What are we gonna do?

                    STEPHEN
          Maybe... Like -- Make up some crazy story of
          why she can't be at the press junket, and the
          premiere.

Stephen snorts the line of cocaine.

                        PATRICIA
          Like, what kind of story?

INT. ALICIA'S BEDROOM - DAWN (DUKE'S SCRIPT)

Duke awakes to find the bed empty next to him. Alicia and
her suitcases are gone.

                        DUKE
          Alicia?

EXT. SANTA MONICA BEACH - DAY - SAME TIME (DUKE'S SCRIPT)

Sandpipers dig for crabs. A wave rolls in as the birds
scamper. In the distance, a man finishes a jog. It's...

sweaty, tan Walters in jog shorts, T-shirt, and fanny
pack. He pulls his phone from the fanny pack. Looks at the
screen.

                        WALTERS
                (into phone)
          Good morning.

INTERCUT PHONE CONVERSATION: EVAN ZUCKER'S OFFICE/BEACH

Zucker stands looking out at the view of the Hollywood
sign.

                        ZUCKER
          So. I had a private detective look into that
          problem patient you told me about... That
          actress doesn't exist.

                        WALTERS
          What do you mean? She stars in movies. She's
          real. I didn't make her up. You met her.

                        ZUCKER
          Be that as it may. There is no legal record of
          her... Anyway, who is real? What is real?...
          Maybe all is not what it seems... Like a dream
          within a dream.

Zucker hangs up as he gazes out at the Hollywood sign.

BEACH

Walters remains on the phone.

                        WALTERS
          What?... Hello?... Hello?

Walters stares at the phone.

                    WALTERS
        The hell?

Left to wonder, he returns the phone to the fanny pack.

EXT. WALTERS' ENTRANCE GATE - MOMENTS LATER (DUKE'S SCRIPT)

Sweat-drenched Walters approaches the security gate. Enters the code, pauses to appreciate a female jogger who passes.

WALTERS' DOORSTEP

Walters removes his sweaty shirt as he walks to the main entrance, and the side of the house. Enters a security code, opens the door.

Alicia emerges from behind a hedge. Jabs a syringe into his neck.

He spins to look. The syringe stuck in his neck.

                    WALTERS
        What are you doing?

She kicks him backwards.

He nearly falls. Grabs hold of the doorway to keep balance.

She jabs a syringe into his back. He turns and barely swipes at her as he loses balance.

                    ALICIA
        A little anesthesia, doctor?

He falls into the doorway.

INT. WALTERS' HOUSE FOYER - SECONDS LATER (DUKE'S SCRIPT)

Alicia drags face down Walters by his wrists. Lets go.

He attempts to grab her ankle. She kicks him. He loses his grip and struggles to crawl.

She casually closes the door. Turns to watch him.

                    WALTERS
            (struggles to crawl)
        What drug is this?

He weakly pulls the phone from his fanny pack. She kicks it away.

                    ALICIA
Who you gonna call? Your lawyer buddy? Scum.

                    WALTERS
              (more drugged)
What drug is this?

                    ALICIA
Shut. Up.

INT. DR. LINDER'S KITCHEN - DAY (DUKE'S SCRIPT)

As she pours coffee, Linder has a phone to her ear.

                    LINDER
              (into phone)
I can't answer your questions. Unless we have
significant reason to believe that she is in
trouble, we can't be calling the police.

She listens.

**INTERCUT PHONE CONV.: STEPHEN'S OFFICE/LINDER'S KITCHEN
(DUKE'S SCRIPT)**

Phone to ear, stressed Stephen stares out the window at
traffic passing.

                    STEPHEN
              (into phone)
What about her parents, where do they live?

                    LINDER
Her parents are dead.

                    STEPHEN
Where did she grow up?

                    LINDER
She never said.

                    STEPHEN
You never asked? That's outrageous.

                    LINDER
When a client is ready to share information,
they provide it.

Stephen simply hangs up the phone.

LINDER'S KITCHEN

Linder puts the phone down. Thinks. Picks up a coffee mug.

STEPHEN'S OFFICE - CONT. (DUKE'S SCRIPT)

Toby enters.

> **TOBY**
> Sharon's on the phone.

Stephen snorts cocaine from a tiny spoon.

> **STEPHEN**
> Sharon who?

> **TOBY**
> Really? Think. Sharon Grock. The director of
> Alicia's film. Hello?

> **STEPHEN**
> Just get out! OUT! GET OUT! NOW!

Toby exits. Slams the door.

Stephen puts on a happy face. Hesitantly picks up the
phone.

> **STEPHEN**
> (into phone)
> Hello, Sharon. I'm glad you--

Holds the phone from his ear as shouting is heard.

I./E. PORSCHE (MOVING)/ALICIA'S STREET - DAY (DUKE'S SCRIPT)

Disheveled, angry, boyish SHARON GROCK (40s), slowly
drives as she looks at...

Home addresses.

Sharon stops at Isabella's old mansion.

INT. ALICIA'S LIVING ROOM - DAY (DUKE'S SCRIPT)

The phone rings.

Wicked cuddles next to Duke asleep on the sofa, his drool
seeps onto a pillow.

> **ALICIA/ANSWERING MACHINE (V.O.)**
> Hello, beautiful person. Leave a message.

> **STEPHEN/ANSWERING MACHINE (V.O.)**
> Alicia, Sharon is quite angry you aren't
> participating in promoting her film. She asked
> for your address. I didn't know what to say.
> Just letting you know. I'm really appalled by

your unprofessional behavior. You really
screwed us. Bye, Alicia.

POUNDING. Duke jolts awake to more POUNDING on the door.

> **SHARON (O.S.)**
> Alicia! You in there?! It's Sharon!

Duke scrambles to peek through a crack in the curtains.

OUTSIDE

Angry Sharon stands at the door.

> **SHARON**
> Who the hell do you think you fucking are? You
> better fucking show up to the fucking premiere,
> you cunt. I swear, I will fucking find you, and
> I will fucking hurt you. You fucking bitch!

Isabella approaches in garish makeup, frumpy gown,
brandishes a golden awards statue as if it's a weapon.

> **ISABELLA**
> Get off of my property!

Isabella threateningly steps forward.

Sharon speedily walks off. Brandishing the gold statue,
Isabella follows her.

> **SHARON**
> What the fucking hell is this shit? Sweet Baby
> Jane?

Sharon gets in her Porsche, starts it, peels out of the
driveway.

Isabella sneers as she watches Sharon drive away.

INT. ALICIA'S BATHROOM - CONT. (DUKE'S SCRIPT)

Duke reads a note taped to the mirror and notices the sink
is filled with stacks of cash.

LIVING ROOM

Duke quickly puts on shoes. Grabs the motorcycle helmet.

INT. WALTERS' RECEPTION - DAY (DUKE'S SCRIPT)

A woman in casual workout clothes and no makeup stands
with a friend at the desk, where Robin sits concerned.

> ROBIN

He's always here at eight a.m. This is so
unlike him.

The phone rings. Robin quickly grabs it.

> ROBIN
> (into phone)

Good morning, Lotus Cosmetic Surgery.

Robin seems relieved, nods her head, smiles at the
patient.

> ROBIN
> (into phone)

Yes... Oh. Okay. I will.

Robin presses the hold button, stands.

> ROBIN

Excuse me. It's the doctor.

Robin quickly exits to...

OFFICE - MOMENTS LATER

Robin on the phone, concern etches her face.

> ROBIN
> (into phone)

Is it the stomach flu?...

INT. WALTERS' HOUSE FOYER - CONT. (DUKE'S SCRIPT)

The point of a knife close to Walters' eye. The black
leather hood has the nostrils and eyes uncovered. The
mouth unzipped.

> WALTERS
> (into phone)

Cancel everything. For a week.

Alicia kneels beside him as she holds the knife to his eye
and phone to his ear. He's on the floor in the bondage
suit, arms Velcroed to his chest.

INTERCUT: WALTERS' OFFICE/HOUSE FOYER (DUKE'S SCRIPT)

Concerned Robin on the phone.

> ROBIN
> (whispers into phone)

Is this about Alicia?

82

                    WALTERS
            (into phone)
     Yes.

                    ROBIN
            (whispers into phone)
     Should I call the police?

WALTERS' FOYER - END INTERCUT

                    WALTERS
            (into phone)
     Absolutely not. I'll be fine.

                    ALICIA
            (whispers)
     Do. Not. Fuck. Up.

                    WALTERS
            (into phone)
     I'll talk with you tomorrow.

Alicia hangs up. Zips shut the mouth on the bondage suit
as he angrily mumbles, his eyes angry.

INT. WALTERS' OFFICE RECEPTION - CONT. (DUKE'S SCRIPT)

Kathy, in surgery scrubs watches worried Robin enter.

The woman patient and her friend wait.

                    ROBIN
     He says he has the flu. I'm sorry, we have to
     cancel the surgery.

The patient and her friend are dumbfounded.

EXT. SANTA MONICA'S PALISADES PARK - DAY (DUKE'S SCRIPT)

Duke dismounts his motorcycle on the street. Runs across
the park grass to...

the cliffside concrete fence. He looks down to see...

P.C.H./WALTERS' BEACH HOUSE

Traffic clogs the southbound lanes. Northbound traffic is
lighter.

PALISADES PARK

Duke at the concrete fence watches...

WALTERS' DRIVEWAY

Alicia's car is parked in the open garage. She exits the garage as the door rolls down. She approaches Walters' Mercedes parked in the short driveway.

PALISADES PARK

Duke steps up onto the concrete fence.

> **DUKE**
> (shouts)
> ALICIA!

WALTERS' DRIVEWAY/P.C.H.

Alicia gets into the driver side of Walters' Mercedes. Door closes. She pulls out into northbound traffic.

PALISADES PARK

Duke runs to his motorcycle. Hops on, tosses on the helmet, starts the engine, speeds away.

E./I. P.C.H. - MALIBU/WALTER'S MERCEDES - DAY (DUKE'S SCRIPT)

Walters' car drives along the scenic coast. Windows down. Rock music blares. Alicia in sunglasses at the wheel.

INT. CAR TRUNK DARKNESS - CONT. (DUKE'S SCRIPT)

The rock music blares. Walters' freaked-out eyes barely seen in the dark. He is in the hooded bondage suit. The mouth zipped closed.

EXT. SANTA MONICA CANYON ROAD - CONT. (DUKE'S SCRIPT)

A street construction crew has the roadway closed.

Duke sits on the motorcycle, stuck in the tangled traffic.

EXT. P.C.H. GAS STATION - LATER - DAY (DUKE'S SCRIPT)

An irritated customer gasses up their car as rock music blares from the Mercedes parked at the next pump. The customer watches...

STORE: Alicia in sunglasses and hat exits. Frantically searches her pockets. Runs back into the store.

INT. GAS STATION STORE - CONT. (DUKE'S SCRIPT)

The cashier is busy with customers.

Panicked Alicia barges in, looks around on the floor.

Customers notice.

                    ALICIA
          Anyone seen my keys?

She searches the counter. Customers also look around.
She runs out.

INT. MERCEDES BACK SEAT - CONT. (DUKE'S SCRIPT)

Rock music blares. Suitcases are in the back seat. The
seat shivers from pounding inside the trunk.

GAS STATION

The curious customer pumping gas watches...

Alicia look around on the pavement. She sees the...

keys on the ground by the car. She snags them. Hops in the
car.

The Mercedes speeds from the gas station.

The customer watches.

I./E. MERCEDES TRUNK/ROAD OFF P.C.H. - DAY (DUKE'S SCRIPT)

In the darkness of the trunk, music blares as Walters'
eyes look around. The trunk opens. Sunlight hits his
masked face as he squints.

                    ALICIA
          Lecherous fuck!

She jabs a syringe into his thigh. He hollers inside the
mask as his panicky eyes bulge.

She punches him. His muffled hollers simmer down.
She slams the trunk. Gets in the car.

A Highway Patrol car pulls up beside her. A kind-of-hot
male OFFICER lowers his window.

She notices him. Silences the music. Rolls down the
window.

                    ALICIA
               (flirty smile)
          Hello.

                    OFFICER
          Everything okay?

> ALICIA

Oh, yeah. Had to take a phone call. Can't talk
on the phone and drive. It's against the law.

> OFFICER
> (charmed)

Where're you headed?

> ALICIA

Up near Monterey. To visit family.

They consider each other.

> ALICIA
> (flirty smile)

If I didn't have a boyfriend.

He snickers.

> ALICIA

Well. I better be on my way.

She shifts into drive.

> OFFICER

Enjoy your drive.

She gives a flirty wave and smile. Casually drives away.

His smile lingers.

INT. ALICIA'S LIVING ROOM - DAY (DUKE'S SCRIPT)

Duke with phone to ear paces.

**INTERCUT: GREGORY'S KITCHEN/ALICIA'S LIVING ROOM (DUKE'S
SCRIPT)**

Gregory stands with phone to ear.

> GREGORY
> (into phone, confused)

The doctor who worked on the movie? Have they
been dating?

> DUKE
> (into phone)

No! He did eyelid surgery on her, and it got
all screwed up.

> GREGORY

My god. That's what this is about?

> DUKE

Yes! That's what I'm saying.

                    GREGORY
This is really a lot of crazy stuff, Duke. She
was driving his car?

                    DUKE
I swear, I'm telling the truth.

                    GREGORY
You haven't called the police?

                    DUKE
No.

                    GREGORY
I'm the only one who you've told?

                    DUKE
Yes. Nobody else knows.

                    GREGORY
If this is true, you have to report it. Or, you
could be considered an accomplice to a crime.

Duke deflates into a chair as he takes that in.

INT. DR. LINDER'S OFFICE - DAY (DUKE'S SCRIPT)

Concerned Linder, phone to ear as she mildly paces.

                    LINDER
Where are you?

INTERCUT: BIG SUR ROADSIDE CLIFF/LINDER'S OFFICE

In sunglasses and hat, Alicia with phone to ear looks down
the cliff to the crashing waves.

                    ALICIA
A beautiful place.

                    LINDER (O.S.)
Do you feel safe?

                    ALICIA
Safe is a matter of perception.

                    LINDER
When can we schedule another appointment?

Alicia steps closer to the edge of the cliff. Muffled
hollering is heard. She turns to look at...

the Mercedes parked nearby.

She considers the distance from the car to the cliff. She hangs up the phone.

DR. LINDER'S OFFICE

Phone still to ear, Linder stands concerned.

> **LINDER**
> (into phone)
> Alicia? Alicia? Hello?

Frustrated. She clicks off the phone.

> **LINDER**
> Bitch! Make an appointment. I have bills to pay.

She kicks the sofa.

> **LINDER**
> Psycho actresses. Who the fuck raises these people?

EXT. WALTERS' MEDICAL BUILDING - DAY (DUKE'S SCRIPT)

Gregory stands on the sidewalk as he looks up to the address.

INT. WALTERS' OFFICE LOBBY - DAY (DUKE'S SCRIPT)

Fish swim around in the wonderful, new tank.

The door opens. Gregory enters. Glances around the empty waiting room.

Flustered Robin sits at the reception desk, phone to ear.

> **ROBIN**
> (into phone)
> Yes... They're handling all of his patients.

She acknowledges Gregory.

> **ROBIN**
> (into phone)
> ... Yes, I know it's an inconvenience, this isn't normal for him... I'm sorry.

She hangs up. Forces a smile.

> **GREGORY**
> Hi. Is the doctor in?

> **ROBIN**
> No. He's -- away. Can I help you?

                    GREGORY
          I'm a friend. Will he be here today?

                      ROBIN
          He's not in town.

                    GREGORY
          Where'd he go?

                      ROBIN
                (doubtful)
          You're a friend of Dr. Walters?

                    GREGORY
          No. Of Alicia Dover.

Her composure goes dark as she stands.

                    GREGORY
          She's a patient here, right?

                      ROBIN
          I don't know. But even if she were...

He waits as she casually grasps the phone and eyes him.

                    GREGORY
          When can I speak with the doctor?

                      ROBIN
          You're going to have to leave.

They stare at each other.

                      ROBIN
          Sir. I will call the police.

                    GREGORY
          Call them.

                      ROBIN
          Get out! GET THE HELL OUT OF HERE!

                    GREGORY
                (backs away)
          It's okay. I'll call the police.

He tosses up his hands as he backs away, and exits.

She runs to the door, locks it.

INT. POLICE OFFICE - DAY (DUKE'S SCRIPT)

A mix of bored and displeased people in line behind
Gregory, who stands at the counter before a YOUNG OFFICER.

                    YOUNG OFFICER
And, your relationship with the missing person?

                       GREGORY
She's my girlfriend. I mean, sort of. Not...
officially.

                    YOUNG OFFICER
Her name?

                       GREGORY
Alicia Dover.

                    YOUNG OFFICER
            (lights up)
The actress? The one in that movie that's
coming out?

                       GREGORY
Yeah. She's in that.

                    YOUNG OFFICER
            (quietly)
I've been trying to break into the industry.
I'm writing screenplays.

                       GREGORY
Oh, yeah?

An older, GRUFF OFFICER (40s), approaches and does
paperwork on the counter. Young Officer gets serious.

                    YOUNG OFFICER
            (to Gregory)
What makes you think she's missing?

                       GREGORY
She's -- Or, her doctor -- Or, both. Seem to
be. Missing.

Gruff Officer keeps an eye on the exchange.

                       GREGORY
It's difficult to explain. The doctor isn't in
his office. And --

                    YOUNG OFFICER
-- Are you his patient?

                       GREGORY
I know this doesn't sound right.

Gruff Officer lets out a mocking snicker.

                    GRUFF OFFICER
              (to anyone)
          It's a full moon tonight.

Young Officer smirks.

                    GREGORY
          Okay. Whatever.

Gregory turns and walks toward the door.

                    GRUFF OFFICER
          Not so fast. Do you have some I.D.?

Gregory stops. Turns. People in line watch.

                    GREGORY
          Yes.

                    GRUFF OFFICER
          May we see it?

Gregory removes his wallet. Hands over the license.

Gruff Officer stares at Gregory. Young Officer slips the
license into a scanner. Gruff Officer takes the license,
hands it back to Gregory.

                    GRUFF OFFICER
          Thank you.

Gregory returns the license to his wallet.

Gruff Officer nods at him.

Gregory nods. Exits.

The next unhappy person in line steps to the counter.

EXT. BIG SUR OCEAN - DAY (DUKE'S SCRIPT)

The sun peeks through tremendous clouds as its rays beam
across the vast ocean.

Billowing water forms waves that glide the surface and
crash against rocky coast.

CLIFFSIDE

Highway One winds along the cliffs where, on a wild
hairline turn, Walters' Mercedes makes its way north.

EXT. BIG SUR CLIFF - DAY (DUKE'S SCRIPT)

Alicia in sunglasses, phone to ear, looks out at the ocean. The Mercedes is parked nearby.

>   ALICIA
>   (into phone)
>   Just thinking I should call you.

INTERCUT: STEPHEN'S OFFICE/BIG SUR CLIFF (DUKE'S SCRIPT)

Toby watches...

Stephen leans over the speaker phone.

>   STEPHEN
>   Where are you? They need you at the premiere
>   tonight. You have to be there, Alicia. You are
>   the star.

>   ALICIA
>   I won't be.

>   STEPHEN
>   Please, don't fuck this up. Toss on a dress and
>   be there. Please!

Alicia looks over the steep cliff, and gazes at the parked Mercedes.

>   STEPHEN
>   Alicia?

She hangs up. Looks over the cliff to the crashing surf.

STEPHEN'S OFFICE

Stephen paces.

>   STEPHEN
>   Fuck!

>   TOBY
>   Well, that's stressful. Maybe time for you to
>   do another bump.

Toby exits.

Stephen lividly stares at the doorway. He takes out the little cocaine box.

>   STEPHEN
>   Can't fire him. Can't strangle him. Can't make
>   him suck my cock.

He takes a dip of the cocaine, but drops the box.

He scampers to his knees. Sniffs cocaine from the rug. Then, licks and licks the rug.

DOORWAY: Delighted Toby takes photos of...

Stephen as he licks the rug.

EXT. BIG SUR FOREST - GRAVEL DRIVEWAY - DAY (DUKE'S SCRIPT)

A rake forms straight lines in the gravel. The rake passes a puddle that reflects the forest. The rake is used by...

LEONARD DOVER (40), in raggedy clothes, old beyond his years. Messy hair. He stops, listens. Turns to see...

the Mercedes approach as it drives along the gravel.

> **LEONARD**
> (scowls)
> No! Not allowed here! NOT ALLOWED!

His scowl fades as his expression brightens.

> **LEONARD**
> Alicia. It's Alicia. Hi, Alicia.

Alicia rolls down the window as she stops near him.

> **LEONARD**
> If I rake the gravel, I can tell if someone's has here been.

> **ALICIA**
> Been here. Move over, Leonard.

Leonard steps aside.

Alicia drives on.

He looks at the tire marks in the gravel. Frustrated, he rakes the gravel to erase the tire marks.

E./I. RAMSHACKLE HOUSE/MERCEDES - CONT. (DUKE'S SCRIPT)

The house sits next to a meadow surrounded by forest. The Mercedes stops in front.

Alicia turns off the engine. She tiredly stares out at... the house and silent forest.

Dread drapes Alicia's face as Walters' muffled hollers are heard from the trunk.

GRASS ALONGSIDE HOUSE - MINUTES LATER

Walters' frantic bloodshot eyes look around as his muffled pleas are heard through the zipped mask of the bondage suit. He is being dragged by a rope tied around his ankles.

Alicia struggles with the rope to the side of the house, she drops it. Pulls open two slanted doors to the basement.

>   ALICIA
> Scream all you want. Nobody can hear you.

Confused Leonard meanders over. Stops and curiously observes Walters.

Walters' angry voice is muffled by the mask as his angry eyes bulge.

>   LEONARD
> What? Why are you dressed like that? Are you a surfer?

Walters' bloodshot eyes factor him.

>   LEONARD
> Are you dad? Alicia, is he our dad?

Alicia grasps Walters' ankles and pulls him to the edge of the slanted doors to the basement.

>   LEONARD
> Did you find him in the ocean?

>   ALICIA
> Leonard, help me push him in.

To Walters' muffled pleas, Leonard hesitantly bends down, and helps Alicia push him into the basement. A thud.

Alicia closes the slanted doors.

INT. DUKE'S APARTMENT - EVENING (DUKE'S SCRIPT)

Duke with phone to ear, stands at the window.

>   DUKE
>   (into phone)
> I don't understand, either.

INTERCUT: GREGORY'S LIVING ROOM/DUKE'S APT. (DUKE'S SCRIPT)

Phil and Nancy eat on the sofa as they watch T.V.

                    PHIL
            (RE: the T.V. screen)
There she is again! Another commercial for her
movie. Damn. She's gonna be famous.

Gregory with phone to ear sits at the dining table.

                  GREGORY
            (into phone)
Unless there's something you aren't telling me,
maybe things aren't as they appear. Maybe
you're imagining some of this. After all,
you're a screenwriter, right?

Phil looks to Gregory and makes the crazy sign: twirls a
finger by his head.

Gregory turns away.

                    DUKE
I'm not imagining it! I'm freaking out. What
can we do?

                  GREGORY
There's nothing I can do.

                    DUKE
Can I call you, if I find out anything?

END INTERCUT: GREGORY'S APARTMENT

Gregory rolls his eyes. Impatiently exhales.

                  GREGORY
Of course. See you, buddy.

Gregory hangs up. Exits.

                    PHIL
            (to Nancy)
That's what he gets for dating an actress.

Gregory reenters.

                  GREGORY
Try being considerate. I liked her.

                    PHIL
Sorry. Sorry, bro. Sorry.

                  GREGORY
You need to move out next week.

Nancy looks to Phil.

                              PHIL
                         (to Nancy)
          It's okay. His son needs the bedroom. I've
          known for months.

Gregory exits. Nancy diverts her eyes to the T.V.

                              PHIL
                         (nudges her)
                Do you need a roommate?

She awkwardly giggles as she watches T.V. He side-eyes
her. She keeps her eyes on the T.V. He ponders.

EXT. P.C.H. NORTH VENTURA COUNTY - NIGHT (DUKE'S SCRIPT)

Duke in the battered helmet rides the motorcycle as the
moon shimmers on the ocean beyond him.

INT. BIG SUR HOUSE BEDROOM - NIGHT (DUKE'S SCRIPT)

A lit candle sits on a side table of the cluttered room.

Alicia, in sunglasses, sits on the bed and injects her
arm. She pulls out the needle, tosses it to the corner.

BASEMENT - LATER (DUKE'S SCRIPT)

TOP OF STAIRS: The door creaks open. Light drifts in.

Barefooted Alicia lazily descends the creaky staircase. In
sunglasses, she drinks from a wine bottle.

A rope tied to a ceiling beam is around Walters' neck. The
mouth zipped on the bondage suit. His bloodshot eyes watch
her. His wrists and forearms are duct taped to the arms of
a chair at the center of the earthen-floored cellar.

She approaches. Stops. Giggles. Swigs from the wine
bottle.

She unzips the mouth of his bondage mask.

                            WALTERS
                Please, let me go.

                            ALICIA
                         (teasingly)
          Go? Go where? Where're you gonna go?

                            WALTERS
                I can arrange to have your eyes repaired.

She huffs as she steps back. Turns. Kicks him in a
shoulder. She nearly falls over.

He winces in pain.

She holds onto the dank wall to balance.

>   **WALTERS**
> Whatever happened to your husband?

She casually circles him.

His reddened eyes watch.

>   **ALICIA**
> His truck flew off the cliff into the ocean.

She stops behind him, he tries to turn to see.

>   **ALICIA**
> They found his truck. Not him. Maybe sharks ate
> him.

She swigs the wine.

>   ALICIA
> Toss things in the ocean here, and who knows
> what happens to them. The fish like food. Do
> you like food? You're not getting any here. I
> hope you're hungry.

She steps in front of him, throws off the sunglasses. Puts
her face up to his, red scars on her eyelids.

>   **ALICIA**
> Look what you did to me.

She backs away.

>   **ALICIA**
> His tire problem was nothing, compared to what
> I'm gonna do to you.

>   **WALTERS**
> What tire problem?

She circles him.

>   **ALICIA**
> I put a spike in his tire. It was nearly flat
> when he sped away. Was so fucking drunk.
> Asshole probably didn't even notice.

She loses balance. Leans against the wall.

>   **WALTERS**
> Why did you spike his tire?

                              ALICIA
              He hit me. For seven years. He bruised my face.
              You bruised my face. You ruined my face.

She sits on the floor. Swigs the wine. Drops the bottle.

                              ALICIA
              He was beautiful... Long blond hair... I liked
              when he walked around naked.

She brushes hair from her face as mud smears her forehead.

She rises and steps over to a dark corner, where there is
a tool bench.

                              ALICIA
              You love playing the piano?

She picks up a small sledgehammer.

Turns to him.

                              ALICIA
              My movie premieres tonight. I was gonna be the
              center of attention. I'm a movie star.

She circles him as she grips the hammer.

                             WALTERS
              I'm sorry, Alicia.

That halts her.

                              ALICIA
                   (glares at him)
              It's so pathetic when people who aren't sorry
              open their mouths and apologize.

                             WALTERS
              Please stop.

                              ALICIA
              Stop? My eyelids don't stop. You did this to
              other people. Doctors told me. They fucking
              hate you.

She hovers the hammer over one of his bound hands.

                             WALTERS
              Please, Alicia. Please, don't.

                              ALICIA
              They said I couldn't sue you. The state medical
              board didn't care, either. The police wouldn't
              arrest you. You have to be stopped.

                    WALTERS
        Please, don't.

                    ALICIA
        Shut the fuck up!

She raises the hammer. His eyes rage with terror.

                    ALICIA
        You molested your patients. Was it fun? This is
        fun for me. And, fuck you if you can't take a
        joke.

She lets out a deranged giggle.

                    WALTERS
        NO!

She smashes the hammer onto his hand. He screams soul-
wrenching pain.

She raises the hammer. Smashes his other hand. His voice
stops. His head slumps, held up by the rope. Fainted.

She drops the hammer. Falls to her knees.

TOP OF STAIRS: Leonard in his pajamas watches as he sucks
his thumb and rocks back and forth.

BEDROOM - LATER - NIGHT (DUKE'S SCRIPT)

Muddy, drunk, Alicia sits on the bed as she ponders.

Leonard paces the room as he sucks his thumb.

                    LEONARD
        Is he dad? Is he dad, Alicia? Does he know
        mom's gone? Does he?

                    ALICIA
        Leonard. Go to bed.

She reclines onto the bed.

He sucks his thumb as he watches her. Briskly exits.

Alicia closes her eyes. Moans are heard from the...

BASEMENT

Walters opens his bloodshot eyes. Still with the rope
around his neck. Wrists bound to the chair. Moans. Louder.
LOUDER.

HALLWAY

Leonard paces as he licks his palms.

BEDROOM

A candle flame flickers on the nightstand. Walters' painful moans drift up from the basement.

As Alicia sleeps, drool seeps from her mouth.

EXT. BIG SUR HOUSE - NIGHT (DREAMY FLASHBACK - DUKE'S SCRIPT)

Sweaty, disheveled Alicia. Blood drips from an eyelid as she crouches next to the front tire of a battered pickup truck.

She uses the small sledgehammer to pound a spike into the tire. The clang echoes into the woods.

EXT. UNDERWATER - NIGHT (DREAMY FLASHBACK - DUKE'S SCRIPT)

Streams of moonlight shimmer through the heaving ocean among ribbons of translucent kelp. Among the kelp...

long blond hair wafts about. It's of Alicia's dead husband. His expression peaceful. A garibaldi fish stops to observe, then gently swims away.

END FLASHBACK

INT. BIG SUR HOUSE HALLWAY - DAY (DUKE'S SCRIPT)

Muddy-faced Alicia, hair a mess, meanders from the bedroom.

> ALICIA
> (lyrically)
> Are you sleeping? Are you sleeping?

She opens the door to the basement, stoops down to look.

BASEMENT

Alicia bolts down the stairs.

The chair is empty. The noose hangs from the beam.

> ALICIA
> (runs upstairs)
> Leonard!

EXT. BIG SUR HOUSE DRIVEWAY - DAY (DUKE'S SCRIPT)

Leonard rakes the gravel.

Alicia runs up to him.

> ALICIA
> (grasps his shoulders)
> Where is that man?

> LEONARD
> You were mean, Alicia. You were really mean.

Leonard bursts out crying as Alicia notices...

footprints in the gravel, all the way around the bend.

DRIVEWAY - MOMENTS LATER

The Mercedes' tires spin as it speeds down the driveway.

Leonard steps aside as the car speeds past him.

> LEONARD
> (cries oddly)
> Ouchie, Alicia. Ouchie!

He sucks his thumb as he whimpers.

INT./EXT. MERCEDES/HIGHWAY ONE - DAY (DUKE'S SCRIPT)

Alicia idles the car as she rolls down the windows to look out at...

the highway draped in extremely heavy fog.

She half exits the car. Listens.

UP THE ROAD

Fog drifts as it obscures a distant figure who tiredly walks.

Walters' bloodshot eyes look back and forth. He is in Leonard's clothes. He holds his swollen hands to his chest. A vehicle is heard.

He hides behind a bush.

A truck drives along the highway, into the heavy fog.

MERCEDES

The windshield wipers swish mist from the glass as Alicia drives slowly with all of the windows down.

UP THE ROAD

In the fog, Walters stops. Listens. Hears the car. He trots away from the road to a boulder. Hides.

INT. MERCEDES: Livid Alicia slowly drives as she listens.

Walters waits for the car noise to fade. Trots back to the highway. Walks cautiously. Stops. Hears the car.

He trots away into a grassy area

He ducks through a wood-beam fence.

INT. MERCEDES: Alicia slows as she notices...

Walters trot away into the fog-shrouded field.

SIDE OF ROAD: She pulls to the side of the road.

> ALICIA
> Need a ride?

She presses on the gas.

The car breaks through the fence, into the bumpy field. Drives up alongside him as he struggles to trot.

> ALICIA
> Get in the car.

He trips. Falls. Moans in pain as he gets up. Stumbles.

She stops the car and exits.

She opens the passenger door. Runs to him, stands ready to kick-box him.

He struggles to stand.

> ALICIA
> Get in the fucking car.

She kicks him in the chest. He nearly falls back.

She jams her foot into his stomach.

He falls into the open passenger door.

IN THE MERCEDES

Walters struggles to get the transmission into drive. The car moves as his legs hang from the passenger door.

She jumps in the driver's door. She gains control and punches him. He tries to get hold of the seat as his legs hang out the door. She speeds.

He falls from the open door.

FIELD

Walters tumbles into the field as the car speeds into the fog.

MERCEDES TIRES...

skid on the dirt, but only slide.

INSIDE MERCEDES

Alicia presses on the brakes as she SCREAMS.

CLIFF

The car flies from the cliff, and plunges into the ocean.

BENEATH WATER

Alicia is knocked out as the car fills with water.

She awakens, hands flounder in a panic as her floating hair obscures her face.

The car elegantly sinks as she stops moving. Her face calm with her hair floating like a halo.

SIDE OF HIGHWAY ONE - CONT. (DUKE'S SCRIPT)

From the fog-shrouded field, Walters limps. Trips and...

his face hits the wet gravel shoulder of the road.

An old hippie van painted with flowers slows. The window rolls down. At the wheel is Duke's girlfriend, Jennifer.

>   JENNIFER
>   Brother, you okay?

Walters agonizingly turns over, his bloodshot eyes look up to her, his hands bloody and swollen.

>   WALTERS
>   (barely)
>   Help me.

Shock traces her face. She cuts the engine, exits the van.

She frantically waves down a car. It slows and pulls over.

HIGHWAY ONE - LATER - DAY (DUKE'S SCRIPT)

The fog has cleared. Several vehicles are stopped.

People tend to...

an incoherent Walters as he struggles to sit. His
bloodshot eyes look around.

Jennifer holds a water bottle to his lips. He sips.

EXT./INT. AMBULANCE - MINUTES LATER (DUKE'S SCRIPT)

E.M.T.s roll the gurney with Walters on it into the
ambulance and secure it to the brace clips.

EXT. AMBULANCE - CONT. (DUKE'S SCRIPT)

The ambulance lights flash and siren turns on as it speeds
up the highway. A helicopter is heard.

A few highway patrol cars are parked as their lights
twirl.

C.H.P. officers do paperwork near another ambulance.

People are on cell phones. All watch as...

the helicopter lands in the field.

HELICOPTER (LANDED)

Emergency workers hop out.

They remove a stretcher with a blanket-covered body.

NEAR THE CARS

Exhausted, Duke cries beside his motorcycle. Jennifer
approaches.

                    JENNIFER
       Did you know her?

He nods as he cries deeply.

                    JENNIFER
       (hugs him)
   I'm so sorry. What's your name?

He cries unconsolably in her arms as she holds him
tightly.

                    DUKE
               (ferociously cries)
     I tried. I tried. Oh my God. I tried... I tried
     to save her.

She continues to hold him as he cries. It's too much as he
loses strength and goes to his knees and all fours.

                    DUKE
     Oh my God! She's dead. Oh my God! Oh my God!

She kneels down beside him to rub his back as he heaves in
deep, guttural cries.

EXT. MANHATTAN BEACH BIKE TRAIL - DAY (DUKE'S SCRIPT)

Passing by are random casual bikers, skaters, people
walking.

Sweaty Gregory jogs along, headphones on his ears. Concern
draws his face. He slows to a walk.

               NEWS RADIO ANNOUNCER (V.O.)
     ... She stars in a film "Driven" that premiered
     nationwide this weekend. Authorities said she
     had been wanted...

Gregory stops as he holds the ear buds to listen.

               NEWS RADIO ANNOUNCER (V.O.)
     ... in the disappearance of celebrity cosmetic
     surgeon, Bernard Walters. Her body was
     recovered from the ocean off the Big Sur
     coast...

Gregory falls to his knees in the sand. Stunned.

               NEWS RADIO ANNOUNCER (V.O.)
     The doctor was airlifted to a hospital in
     Monterey...

Gregory bursts in tears.

People dismissively glance as they pass by.

EXT. OCEAN WATER/SANTA MONICA PIER - DAY (DUKE'S SCRIPT)

Flowers land on the billowing water that glistens with
sun.

END OF PIER

Gregory contemplates the ocean. He holds the hand of a
young boy, his son. Gregory leads the boy off into the
crowds of tourists and street performers.

EXT. ISABELLA'S FRONT YARD - DAY (DUKE'S SCRIPT)

Humorously aghast news reporters and camera crews stand on the sidewalk. Their cameras and microphones point to...

Isabella, wig askew, makeup garishly done. She wears an old gown. Holds a puppy dressed in a tutu and with eye makeup.

> **ISABELLA**
> (the puppy licks her face)
> Yes, that's a lovely puppy. Mummy adores you, too. Oh, yes, yes.

Isabella smiles at each camera, as if on a red carpet.

> **ISABELLA**
> I knew the cameras would be here for me, one day.

The news crew exchange creepily humored glances.

INT. STEPHEN'S OFFICE - DAY (DUKE'S SCRIPT)

Stephen sits at the desk, phone to ear.

> **STEPHEN**
> (into phone)
> Devastated... Just as her career was going to fly...

Near him, Patricia stares out at traffic on Wilshire Blvd.

> **STEPHEN**
> (into phone)
> She willed everything to some background extra, struggling screenwriter, or whatever... I know, what a waste... But... Well -- The doctor might participate in a book and film deal... If they cut him a piece of the back end... So greedy. Some people, you wonder who raised them -- Oh, get this! Larry Valsa said she was the love of his life --

Toby steps forward, presses the hang-up button on the phone.

> **STEPHEN**
> What. The. Fuck.

Toby happily holds up an enlarged photo of Stephen licking cocaine from the rug.

Stephen grabs the photo and rips it to pieces.

                        TOBY
                 (unfazed)
          I've been promoted. I'm an agent now. Like you.
          How fun, huh? Be nice. I have copies of that
          photo.
Stephen and Patricia watch as Toby exits.

                      PATRICIA
          What was that photo of?

                      STEPHEN
                 (glares at the door)
          Patricia. Shut up. This time, just shut up.

She is aghast.

EXT. BIG SUR HOUSE - DAY (REAL LIFE)

Sweaty Duke works on replacing a plank on the porch stairs
of the house that is much less rickety, but is well-cared
for.

Jennifer exits the front door with a tall glass of water.
Hands it to him. He guzzles it.

                      JENNIFER
          This is a great place to finish writing my
          novel. And for you to finish another
          screenplay.

She sits in a chair, where she pets Wicked the cat.

                      JENNIFER
          Maybe we can start a writers' retreat up here.

Alicia exits the house. A screenplay in her hand. The scar
still on her eyelid. Exchanges a humored glance with Duke.

                        DUKE
Did you read it?

Alicia sits on the porch sofa as she flips through the
script. Stops at a page.

Duke sits next to her as he lights a joint. Tokes. Hands
her the joint.

                       ALICIA
                 (takes the joint)
          I like how you gave us all roles.

She hits the joint. Duke watches and waits.

                    ALICIA
              (exhales smoke)
         So twisted.

Duke and Jennifer laugh with Alicia.

                    ALICIA
         My mom murdered my father, I murdered my ex-
         husband, I torture a doctor. Then, I die?

                    DUKE
         You encouraged me to write a screenplay.

Alicia hits the joint again, hands it to Jennifer, who
tokes. Duke and Alicia share a laugh.

                    ALICIA
              (exhales smoke)
         The scar is from falling out of a tree when I
         was five. It doesn't bother me.

                    DUKE
         It shouldn't. Dudes dig scars.

Alicia and Jennifer giggle.

                    JENNIFER
         Good save.

                    ALICIA
         It would be good to change Larry's name. He's a
         vindictive scumbag.

Duke stares out at the trees.

                    JENNIFER
         His mind's ticking.

                    DUKE
         What about... Are there any scumball producers
         named Harvey?

Alicia snickers as she flips through the script.

                    ALICIA
         I want to show this to my manager.

Jennifer winks at Duke.

                    ALICIA
         For the record, I didn't have sex with Larry
         Valsa.

                    DUKE
         For the record, define sex.

They laugh. Alicia places the script down, gives him a look, runs out to...

the yard, where she catches a Frisbee, and spins it off to...

Gregory, who tosses it to...

his son.

DRIVEWAY

Leonard rakes the gravel. He pauses to observe his work as he rocks back and forth and sucks his thumb.

PORCH

In raggedy hippy clothes and messy hair, Alicia sits gazing at the forest. Her eyelid scar obvious.

In a nearby chair, her hippy Mom sits peeling an apple, cuts it into pieces, tosses it into a bowl. Starts peeling another. She notices...

Alicia gazing at the woods.

>   **MOM**
>   Whatchya' thinkin' about, honey?

Alicia slightly giggles.

>   **ALICIA**
>   Thinking of... maybe... writin' a screenplay.

>   **MOM**
>   Oh. Give it a try. You always did like movies.

Mom peels another apple as Alicia sits thinking.

Leonard, in different clothes and with a better haircut exits the front door. Sits on the sofa beside Alicia.

>   **LEONARD**
>   Pickup truck has a flat. Looks like a spike got
>   in the tire. Don't know how that happened. I'll
>   change it after diner.

He watches Mom peel apples, as Alicia stares.

>   **LEONARD**
>   (to Alicia)
>   Remember that time you fell outa the apple
>   tree? So much blood everywhere.

Alicia stares.

                    LEONARD
          You know, there's doctors who can get rid of
          that scar.

Mom gives Leonard a cautionary glance.

Alicia clicks out of her stare, looks to Leonard as if
he's being absurd.

                    ALICIA
          Why would I do that? It doesn't bother me.

Leonard glances at Mom, who gently shakes her head "no."

Leonard shrugs.

And Alicia continues to gaze out at the forest.

                    THE END

I hope you enjoyed the ride.

And that you can one day watch this film.

The scenes on the silver screen
will be what were at one time my thoughts unseen.

Daniel

The Screenwriter

Daniel John Carey is the founder of the Los Angeles-based Screenwriting Tribe screenplay incubation workshop for writers helping writers.

Carey also is the author of the *Screenplay Repair Manual*. The book has been used as a text in film schools. It was written to go along with David Trottier's *The Screenwriter's Bible*. Those interested in writing screenplays are encouraged to study both books, and apply what they learn to their screenplays, before submitting the screenplays to managers, agents, producers, development executives, and others in the industry.

If you have enjoyed the screenplay,
please write a customer review on Amazon
to entice others to partake.

www.ingramcontent.com/pod-product-compliance
Lightning Source LLC
Chambersburg PA
CBHW081206170626
46811CB00011B/3330